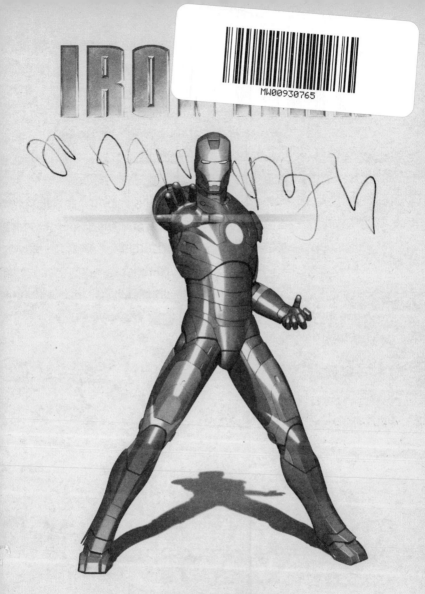

Written by Stephen Sullivan
Based on the Screenplay for 'Iron Man' by
Mark Fergus, Hawk Ostby, Art Marcum & Matt Holloway
Based on the Marvel Comic

CHAPTER 1

A convoy of US Army Humvees moved through the Afghanistan desert, kicking up clouds of dust in their wake.

Tony Stark, genius inventor and billionaire businessman, relaxed in the back of one of the trucks and watched as the bleak landscape rushed past the window. The vehicle was cramped, sweaty, and hot — a far cry from the air-conditioned luxury Tony had known all his life, but he didn't mind. He loosened his tie and settled into the seat, nodding his head to the classic rock blasting out of the stereo.

Tony surveyed the three soldiers riding with him. They sat in awkward silence and the recruit next to Tony kept stealing awestruck glances at his celebrity passenger. Tony looked at them over the top of his sunglasses.

"I feel like you're driving me to a Court Marshall, this is crazy," said Tony. "What, you're not allowed to talk?"

"We can talk, sir," said the soldier next to him, nervously.

"I see, so it's personal," mused Tony.

"No, you intimidate them," corrected the soldier behind the wheel, with a smile.

Tony nearly jumped. "You're a woman!" he blurted.

Buried under their gear, the three soldiers had looked alike to Tony. They all chuckled.

Tony's face reddened as he straightened up in his seat.

"I would apologize, but isn't that what we're going for here? I thought of you as a soldier, first."

"I'm an airman," replied the woman, amused.

"Well, you have excellent bone-structure," said Tony, trying to dig himself out of a hole. "I'm actually having kind of a hard time *not* looking at you now. Is that weird?"

His joke broke the ice and all three soldiers laughed.

Tony laughed too. "Come on, it's OK. Laugh!" he said.

"Is it cool if I take a picture with you?" asked the soldier right next to him, suddenly emboldened. He couldn't wait to get a picture with Tony Stark, head of the very powerful weapons manufacturer, Stark Industries.

"Yes," agreed Tony, "it's very cool."

Grinning, the soldier crowded next to Tony, as his friend in the front seat held up a digital camera.

"OK . . ." said the soldier, as he focused the camera.

Just then, a huge explosion rocked the truck. Tony watched through the windshield as an enormous ball of fire knocked the Humvee ahead of them off the dirt road.

Tony slammed into the side of the truck. His gaze fell on the right sideview mirror just as the Humvee behind them blew up, too.

Trapped between two burning vehicles, Tony's Humvee skidded to a stop. The sound of gunfire rattled the windows.

"What's going on?" said Tony, confused.

The soldiers picked up their guns and jumped out of the car, trying to secure the Humvee's position. Tony watched in horror as they were all shot down instantly.

Suddenly, another explosion rocked the vehicle and burst holes all along one side. Breathing hard, Tony looked desperately out of the windows. All around the Humvee, soldiers were slumped on the ground and the attackers, whoever they were, seemed to be getting closer with each shot. Tony knew he was doomed if he stayed in the Humvee. So he scrambled across the seat and out of the far door.

Tony stumbled across the rugged landscape, looking for cover. Smoke stung his eyes and the sound of gunfire echoed in his head. He crouched behind a rock and pulled out his mobile phone.

Just then, something landed nearby with a soft thud – an unexploded rocket-propelled grenade. Tony gaped at the info stencilled on the side of the explosive: STARK INDUSTRIES.

The enemy was shooting at him with weapons made by his own company! Tony froze.

Please let it be a dud! he thought. *Please let it be –*

A blaze of blinding white light surrounded him as the grenade went off. The blast hurled Tony through the air and he landed hard on the ground. The air rushed out of his lungs. He pulled open his shirt and registered that his chest was bleeding, before the world around him faded away.

When Tony came to, he found himself tied securely to a chair in a dark cave. Ragged, makeshift bandages covered his body. Every part of him hurt – especially his chest. It was all he could do to stay conscious.

Around him stood five scruffy guards, armed with machine guns. On the other side of the cave, a video camera focused on Tony and the group of men. Next to him stood a man reading a prepared statement for the camera in a language Tony didn't understand.

Tony realized the men must be insurgents — the rebel fighters who had attacked his convoy — and they were making some kind of ransom video. Then, he passed out.

CHAPTER 2

Just thirty-six hours earlier, Tony had been safe and sound in the USA – although he was still getting himself into trouble.

On a stage in a large conference room, Colonel James Rhodes, Tony Stark's best friend, had stood clutching an award as a film about Tony's life played on a huge screen. The film showed Tony's privileged childhood, his first-class schooling, and his amazing ability to design and build machines.

"Since inheriting Stark International from his father," the video's narrator marvelled, "Tony has worked on innovative high-tech projects. He designed the experimental Arc Reactor and has created many of the new smart weapons systems that help keep all of us safe. Today, Tony Stark's ingenuity continues to protect freedom and American interests around the world."

As the video came to a close, an inspiring shot of the American flag, waving dramatically, filled the screen. The show ended and the lights came up.

"Ladies and gentlemen," Rhodey said, "it is my honour to present this year's Apogee Award to Mr Tony Stark . . ."

The crowd in the auditorium broke into thunderous applause. All eyes looked to the door, expectantly. But no one emerged. The applause quickly faded into surprised murmurings.

Rhodey gritted his teeth as Obadiah Stane, Stark International's to the stage and took the podium.

 . . . I'm not Tony Stark. But if I were,

 . . . and . . . what a joy it is to receive this

 . . . a deep breath and forced a grin.

 . . . the worst thing — he's always working."

 . . . was, in fact, in a nearby Las Vegas

 . . . table, betting enormous amounts of money. He paused and threw the dice, turning up another winner. The crowd around the table cheered.

Just then, Tony spotted Rhodey striding towards him across the casino floor.

"Rhodey!" Tony exclaimed. "They roped you into this awards thing, too?"

Rhodey scowled at him. "Yeah. They said if I presented you with an award, you'd be deeply honoured."

Tony stood up and straightened his tie. "That's great," he said. "When do we do it?"

Rhodey plopped the award down on the gaming table. Tony stared at it, surprised.

"I'm so sorry," Tony said, not meaning it at all.

Rhodey smiled and shook his head.

Tony picked up the dice, shook them, and rolled — but they came up losers. The crowd around the table sighed and glared at Rhodey, as though he had brought Tony bad luck.

It was time to leave. Tony collected a huge stack of chips from the table and headed for the door. As he passed, people gawked and took pictures of him with their mobile phones.

Tony dumped his award in the hands of a costumed casino employee and was just about to step into his limousine when an attractive woman holding a voice recorder pushed her way through the crowd.

"Mr Stark!" she called. "Christine Everhart, *Vanity Fair*. Can I ask you a few questions?"

"OK, go," Tony replied, turning to answer her.

"You've been described as the da Vinci of our times," Ms Everhart said. "What do you say to that?"

"Ridiculous," Tony said. "I don't paint."

"And what do you have to say about your other nickname: the Merchant of Death?"

Tony rubbed his chin. "That's not bad," he began flippantly, but an icy stare from the reporter stopped him.

"Look," he said, "it's an imperfect world. I guarantee you, the day that weapons are no longer needed to keep the peace, I'll start making bricks and beams to make hospitals."

"Rehearse that line much?" Ms Everhart asked.

"Every night in front of the mirror," said Tony.

She frowned. "All I want is a serious answer."

"Here's serious," he said. "My old man had a philosophy: peace means having a bigger stick than the other guy."

"Good line," she replied, "coming from the guy selling the sticks."

The remark stung. "My father helped defeat Hitler," Tony said, his teeth gritted. "A lot of people — including your magazine bosses — might call that being a hero."

"Others might call it war profiteering."

Tony chuckled. "Tell me, Christine Everhart," he said, "how do you plan to report on the millions of people we've saved by advancing medical technology? Or the millions more we've kept from starving with our intelli-crops? All those breakthroughs were spawned by our military projects."

Without waiting for a reply, Tony turned and left the casino.

CHAPTER 3

Tony Stark's mansion home stood atop a tall cliff on the edge of the Pacific Ocean. The house was a sprawling, ultramodern building — all glass and shining steel. It sat precariously on the edge of the bluff, giving its owner a commanding view of the surf far below.

Tony wasn't admiring the view, though. As usual, he was working in the huge laboratory-garage beneath the mansion. This morning, his project was tuning up one of the cars in his collection, an old '32 Ford. He looked up as an attractive redhead entered the workshop. It was his personal assistant, Virginia 'Pepper' Potts.

"You are supposed to be half-way around the world right now," she said. "Your flight was scheduled to leave an hour and a half ago."

"I thought with it being my plane and all, it would just wait for me to get there," sighed Tony.

Pepper ignored him and forged ahead with her to-do list.

"Tony I need to speak to you about a couple of things before I get you out of here."

She looked at her clipboard. "Do you want to buy the Jackson Pollock painting? The owner has another buyer in the wings."

Tony asked for her opinion.

"Well," she said. "I think it's incredibly overpriced, and —"

"I need it. Buy it," he instructed.

Pepper smiled, ticking it off her list.

"The MIT commencement speech," she said, pressing on. "Yes or no?"

"What are you trying to get rid of me for?" Tony interrupted. He gazed into her eyes. "Have you got plans?"

"As a matter of fact I do," said Pepper. She lifted her perfect nose just slightly. "I'm allowed to have plans on my birthday."

"It's your birthday again?" Tony said.

"Yep," she replied. "Isn't that strange – same day as last year."

"Well, get yourself something nice from me," he said.

"I already did," Pepper answered, smiling indulgently. "Thank you, Mr Stark."

"You're welcome, Ms Potts," replied Tony.

They looked at each other for a moment, before Pepper handed him an espresso and ushered him out of the door.

James Rhodes stood scanning the tarmac for any sign that Tony might be on his way. Behind him, the Stark Industries private jet sat waiting.

Just then, a sports car roared up, a Rolls-Royce limousine right beside it. Tony's chauffeur, "Happy" Hogan, popped open the Rolls' trunk and pulled out Tony's overnight suitcase. Tony hopped out of the car.

Rhodey was fuming. "What's wrong with you?" he bellowed, as Tony headed towards him. "I've been standing out here for three hours!"

"Waiting on you now," Tony said, sliding past him into the plane. "Let's get going. Wheels up – rock 'n' roll!"

Pretty air stewards handed out hot towels as Tony and Rhodey settled into the jet's plush, leather seats. Rhodey buried his head in a newspaper.

"Come on sour patch, don't be mad," teased Tony.

"I'm not mad, I'm indifferent," Rhodey answered, grumpily. "You don't respect yourself, so I know you don't respect me. I'm just your babysitter."

"I respect you. I said I was sorry," Tony said, trying to appease him. He didn't want to argue, and he certainly wasn't in the mood for being serious. "You want a drink?" he asked.

Rhodey shook his head in disbelief. "We're not drinking! We're working right now! You are constitutionally incapable of being responsible."

But Tony was very persuasive. Despite Rhodey's protests, it ended up being a late night.

The next morning, they touched down in Bagram Air Force Base in Afghanistan. Once there, a convoy of Humvees took them from the base to a fortified test site in the desert.

As Rhodey settled in among the army generals and VIPs, Tony went to work. He positioned himself on a huge rock and launched into his speech, boasting the virtues of Stark International's latest equipment.

"The age-old question," Tony said, "is whether it's better to be feared or respected. I say, is it too much to ask for both?"

His eyes gleamed as he walked over to a Jericho missile perched atop a mobile launcher.

"With that in mind," Tony continued, "I humbly present the crown jewel of Stark Industries' Freedom Line of armaments. This is the first missile to incorporate my proprietary repulsor technology — or RT, as we like to call it — a breakthrough in energy control and guidance."

He pressed a button on a remote, and the missile streaked into the air. The rocket arced gracefully towards a nearby rocky mountain peak.

"Let one of these off the chain," Tony said, "and I personally guarantee you, the bad guys won't even want to come out of their caves. For your consideration . . . the Jericho."

He pointed as the Jericho missile divided from a single weapon into a swarm of mini-missiles. The missiles smashed into the nearby peak. With a deafening roar, the mountain exploded into a shower of debris.

Dust washed over Tony and the generals. Tony continued smiling, unfazed by the sudden blast. The generals and Afghani officials nodded and muttered amongst themselves, impressed.

"Gentlemen," Tony said, "Stark International operators are standing by to take your orders." He walked off to answer his mobile phone. Obadiah Stane's face appeared on the video screen.

"Obi!" said Tony.

"How did it go?" Stane asked, eagerly.

Stark grinned. "It went great. Looks like it's going to be an early Christmas."

Tony signed off and stepped into a waiting Humvee. Rhodey followed and went to climb in after him.

"I'm sorry," said Tony, slamming the door before he could get in. He leaned out of the window. "This is the 'Fun-vee'. The 'Humdrum-vee' is back there." He gestured to the vehicle behind him.

"Nice job," said Rhodey, walking dejectedly to the other truck.

The soldiers cranked up the stereo and Tony's Humvee roared off into the desert.

That was the last thing Tony Stark could remember. When he opened his eyes again, he was in some kind of emergency room — though it didn't look like a very good one. He was strapped to a bed and connected to numerous wires and tubes. Everything around him, even the medical equipment, looked dirty and ill-repaired. An ageing man in a doctor's smock stood over a nearby sink, shaving. He didn't notice that Tony had woken up.

Feeling thirsty, Tony reached for a pitcher of water on a nearby table, but it remained beyond his grasp; the tubes and wires connecting him to the medical machines wouldn't let him stretch that far. He grabbed hold of the wires and pulled, trying to rip them out. Somehow, he didn't have the strength. His chest ached terribly.

The doctor noticed his efforts. "I wouldn't do that if I were you," he said in slightly accented English. His dark eyes strayed meaningfully down the wires to a nearby car battery. A chill rushed down Tony's spine. Who were these people? What had they done to him?

He put his hand on his bandaged chest and suddenly remembered everything – the attack, the rebels, the bomb. He was in the hands of the enemy. He'd been taken prisoner. And they'd done something to his heart.

CHAPTER 4

Tony faded in and out of consciousness for a long time. When he could finally focus again, he was in a cave. The doctor stood a dozen yards away, stirring a bubbling pot over a small gas-fired furnace. It looked like he was working on an experiment. Flickering fluorescent lights dangled overhead. A closed metal door seemed to be the room's sole exit. Dirt, grease and blood stained the doctor's yellowed smock. He had a tanned, wrinkled face, grey hair and thick glasses.

Tony moved to sit near the doctor, watching him work over the stove. He wasn't experimenting – he was cooking. Tony examined his chest with a dirty piece of mirror. A bulky metal object protruded from beneath his fresh bandages.

"What have you done to me?" he asked, aghast.

The doctor stopped stirring the pot and chuckled. "What I did is to save your life. I removed all the shrapnel I could, but there's a lot left and it's headed to your atrial septum. Here, wanna see? I have a souvenir."

The man picked up a small glass jar from a shelf and shook it. Tiny barbs of metal rattled around inside. "Take a look," he said, tossing the jar to Tony.

Tony, who was no longer strapped down, caught it and winced. His chest felt very, very strange. He examined the tiny shards of metal in the jar.

"I've seen many wounds like that in my village. We call them the 'walking dead', because it takes about a week for the barbs to reach the vital organs."

Tony was finding it hard to take this in. He looked at his chest plate and felt sick.

"What *is* this?" he asked.

"That is an electromagnet, hooked up to a car battery. It's keeping the shrapnel from entering your heart," smiled the doctor.

Tony looked at the nearby car battery, connected to the wires on his chest, and shuddered. Then he noticed a security camera perched high on the cave wall. They were being watched.

The doctor nodded. "That's right. Smile!"

Somehow, Tony didn't feel like smiling.

"We met once, you know," the doctor continued, stirring the pot, "at a technical conference in Bern, Switzerland."

"I don't remember," Tony said.

"You wouldn't," the man laughed. "For all the partying you did, you gave a surprisingly good lecture on integrated circuits."

Just then, a metal slat in the middle of the door slid back, revealing two menacing eyes.

The doctor stopped stirring. "Stand up!" he hissed at Tony.

He dropped his spoon and helped Tony up.

Before Tony could ask why, the door swung open and a powerful-looking, bearded man entered, flanked by several armed henchmen. The man began speaking in Arabic and the doctor translated. "He says, 'Welcome, Tony Stark, the most famous mass-murderer in the history of America. He is honoured'."

The man held out a surveillance photo showing an image of the

17

Jericho missile test. He continued talking.

"He wants you to build the missile. The Jericho missile that you demonstrated," the doctor translated.

Tony took a deep breath. His chest ached. "I . . . refuse," he said.

The man signalled to his henchmen, who grabbed Tony and pushed his face into a tank of water. He spluttered and gasped as they dunked his head in and out of the water.

Then the men bundled Tony out of the cell, covering his head roughly with a dirty hood. He was dragged along, stumbling across rough and rocky ground, until one of Bakar's henchmen yanked off the hood that was obscuring his vision.

Blinking against the sudden light, Tony found himself in a valley surrounded by tall mountains. He realized that his cell was inside one of the mountains – these people had hewn tunnnels and rooms into the rock. The day's brightness stung his eyes, and it took him a moment to process what he was seeing.

Skids piled with weapons surrounded him. All of the munitions – some dating back twenty years – bore the Stark Industries logo.

The bearded man barked at him.

"He wants to know what you think," the doctor translated, watching Tony's shocked reaction.

"I think you've got a lot of my weapons," Tony answered, grimly.

The man spoke again.

"He says," the doctor translated, "they have everything you need to build the Jericho missile. He wants you to make a list of materials. You will start working immediately." He paused. "And when you are done, he will set you free."

Tony looked at the man, who grinned, holding out his hand.

"No, he won't," Tony said. He smiled through gritted teeth and shook hands with the man.

"No," the doctor agreed quietly. "He won't."

Tony looked around the valley, his eyes settling on a menacing man nearby. He stood atop a rock, surrounded by armed men, watching the proceedings. He was clearly in charge — a warlord.

A few days later Tony, wrapped in an army surplus blanket, sat before the fire in his cell. He stared into the cracking flames with a defeated expression.

The doctor sat next to him. He leaned close and spoke urgently.

"I'm sure your people are looking for you, Stark," he said, "but they will never find you in these mountains."

Tony said nothing.

The doctor's voice grew more desperate. "Look, what you just saw, that is your legacy, Stark — your life's work, in the hands of those murderers! Is that how you want to go out? Is this the last act of defiance of the great Tony Stark, or are you going to do something about it?"

"Why should I do anything?" Tony replied in a whisper. "They're going to kill me, you . . . and either way, even if they don't, I'm going to be dead in a week."

The doctor looked into his eyes. "Well, then, this is a very important week for you, isn't it?"

Tony suddenly had an idea.

CHAPTER 5

Tony's cell was a hive of activity. All around him, men carried weapons and equipment.

Tony made an arc with his hands. "This is going to be my work station," he instructed. "I want it well-lit. I'm going to need welding gear – I don't care if it's acetylene or propane – I need a soldering station, a helmet, goggles, and a smelting cup. I need two sets of precision tools . . ."

The doctor stood beside him, translating Tony's list as fast as he could to the men, who hurried off to fill the requests.

The next day, Tony began salvaging the pieces he needed from the ageing weapons the rebels had brought. The doctor watched him with interest.

"Who are these people?" asked Tony.

"They are your loyal customers, sir," the doctor replied. "They call themselves the Ten Rings."

Tony moved across the workshop and opened one end of a missile with a drill. The doctor followed and crouched down beside him.

"Now, we might be more productive if you include me in the planning process . . ." he suggested.

Tony looked at The doctor. Even after all they'd been through together, could he trust him? Tony decided he could.

He pulled the missile apart and carefully extracted a tiny strip of metal, holding it up to the light with a pair of tweezers.

The doctor looked surprised. "What is that?"

"Palladium," Tony answered. "0.15 grams. We need at least 1.6, so let's go break down the other eleven missiles."

The doctor nodded.

It took hours for the two of them to collect the strips they needed. Tony instructed the doctor to heat the metal strips in the furnace, until they melted, while he made a mould.

When the metal had liquified, the doctor carefully clasped the sides of the smelting cup with a pair of tongs. He slowly lifted it and walked towards Tony's workstation.

"Careful!" warned Tony, nervously. They couldn't afford to waste a single drop.

"Relax! I have steady hands," reassured the doctor. "Why do you think you're still alive, huh?"

The doctor smoothly poured the molten palladium into the mould. As Tony watched his skilful work, he realized he'd never asked the doctor his name.

"What do I call you?" he said.

"Yinsen," replied the doctor.

"Nice to meet you," said Tony.

"Nice to meet you, too," said Yinsen, with a smile.

When the palladium had cooled, Tony lifted it carefully out of the mould. It had formed a fine metal ring. He set the ring inside a small metal circle. Yinsen watched intently.

Tony kept working at the metal circle, twisting copper wire around its edges, soldering, making miniscule movements with his tweezers — it was intricate and complicated work. He kept working around the clock, neither resting nor sleeping.

Finally, Tony finished connecting the last pieces of the device and flicked the lab generator switch. The lights in the cave dimmed and the palm-sized device glowed atop the workbench.

"That doesn't look like a Jericho missile," Yinsen observed.

"That's because it's a miniaturized Arc Reactor," Tony said. "I've got a big one powering my factory at home. Its repulsor technology should keep the shrapnel away from my heart."

"But what can it generate?" asked Yinsen, doubtfully.

"If my math is right – and it always is – three gigajoules per second," Tony replied.

Yinsen's mouth dropped open. "That could run your heart for fifty lifetimes!"

A sly grin crept over Tony's face. "Or something really big for fifteen minutes."

Being careful to avoid the gaze of the surveillance camera, he showed Yinsen the real plans for the project. He had drawn what looked like missile schematics on salvaged pieces of paper – but when they were layered on top of each other, they formed a very different picture. Yinsen's weathered face broke into a smile as he looked at the drawing. It was an articulated metal man.

"Wow!" gasped Yinsen. "Impressive."

Tony installed the glowing reactor in his chest.

Weeks later, Tony and Yinsen sat together in the cell. They'd been hard at work, day and night, constructing the pieces of Tony's plans. Tonight, they were resting up, playing backgammon on a board

22

Yinsen had made.

"You still haven't told me where you're from," mused Tony, as he rolled the dice.

"I'm from a small town called Gulmira," Yinsen replied. "It's actually a nice place."

"Got a family?" Tony asked.

"Yes," said Yinsen, "and I will see them when I leave here. And you, Stark?"

Tony looked at Yinsen, then lowered his eyes. "No."

Yinsen leaned back in his chair. "So, you're a man who has everything . . . and nothing."

Over the following days, the two of them worked feverishly: soldering circuits, connecting electronics, hammering metal — and always trying to conceal their real purpose from the watchful eyes of the enemy.

One evening, Tony was bent over some salvaged sheet metal, cutting, welding, and bending it into shape. The laboratory was strewn with parts that might, for all his captors knew, be assembled into a high-tech missile.

But the guards were starting to get suspicious. As Tony's machine took shape, they observed the workshop through the surveillance cameras.

One of the henchmen held up the photograph of the Jericho missile and compared it to what was being built on screen. "It doesn't look anything like the picture," he said. He went to warn his boss that something was up.

A little later, Tony and Yinsen were experimenting with the glowing

23

repulsor technology in Tony's chest. Tony plugged a long wire into the chest plate and then attached a sensor on the end of the wire to his leg.

Yinsen positioned an electronic contraption that looked like a piece of hinged metal on a tabletop nearby. He nodded and held his breath.

Tony flexed his leg. The glow of his chest plate, which was powering the device, dimmed slightly. The beat-up laptop attached to the device whirred, making the necessary control calculations.

The contraption on the table jumped, moving in the exact same way that Tony's leg had.

The two men looked at each other, triumphant.

But in another room, the warlord was watching them on camera, and he didn't like what he saw.

The door to the lab flew open and the bearded man stormed in, followed by a pack of guards, then the man Tony had observed from the rock. The warlord.

The warlord walked over to Tony, parted his shirt and touched the glowing Arc Reactor in his chest.

"The bow and arrow once was the pinnacle of weapons technology," he mused. "It allowed Genghis Khan to rule from the Pacific to the Ukraine. An empire twice the size of Alexander the Great's and four times the size of the Roman Empire."

He walked to the workbench and looked at the missile schematics Tony had drawn on the pieces of paper.

The warlord fixed his cold eyes on Tony. "Today, whoever has the latest Stark weapons rules these lands. Soon, it will be my turn."

Sensing something was amiss, he turned to Yinsen and spoke in Urdu. "Why have you failed me?" he asked.

24

Yinsen shook his head and replied, "We're working. Diligently."

The warlord paced slowly towards Yinsen. "I let you live . . . and this is how you repay me."

Yinsen looked nervous. "The missile is very complex," he replied. "He's trying very hard."

The warlord glanced at Stark. Tony remained stoic.

At a nod from the warlord, the guards seized Yinsen and forced him to his knees. The warlord turned towards the furnace.

"You think I'm a fool?" the warlord asked. "I'll get the truth."

When he turned to face Yinsen, he was holding a red-hot burning coal between some tongs.

"Open your mouth," he said, menacingly.

The guards forced Yinsen's face down onto an anvil. The warlord moved the coal towards him. "Tell me the truth," he spat.

"He's building the Jericho!" shouted Yinsen.

The warlord kept shouting, "Tell me the truth!" and Yinsen kept giving the same answer.

Tony watched in horror as the coal moved ever closer to Yinsen's face. Suddenly, he stepped forward.

"I need him," said Tony.

The warlord looked up.

"Good assistant," Tony explained.

The warlord looked at him hard. He dropped the coal. "You have until tomorrow to assemble my missile," he said.

He turned and left the room. The others followed, locking the door as they left.

CHAPTER 6

That night, Tony worked tirelessly to finish his secret project. He hammered and welded and sweated, never stopping for a moment.

Finally, he beat the last piece of metal into shape and wiped the soot from his face. He picked up the object and plunged it into the barrel of cold water next to him, then took it over to where Yinsen was sitting, working on some circuitboards. He placed it on the table. It was an iron mask – crude, but it would definitely suit his purpose.

At last, Tony was ready to fit the pieces of his plan together – but they were racing against the clock. Behind a makeshift screen, which shielded their actions from the camera, Tony pulled on a leather shirt and gloves. Yinsen pressed a control button on the lab's winch and lowered a huge, metal chest piece over Tony. As Yinsen used a power drill to seal him inside the suit, Tony connected the armour's electronics.

"Say it again," instructed Yinsen.

"Forty-one steps straight ahead, then sixteen steps left from the door, fork right, thirty-three steps, turn right," Tony replied, running through their carefully-constructed plan, as Yinsen adjusted the hydraulics on his arms.

In the control room, the warlord examined the monitor.

On the screen, which showed Tony and Yinsen's cell, he could see Yinsen working furiously, cutting and welding. Sparks flew, at times obscuring the camera's view. What was he up to?

"Where is Stark?" he barked at the guard next to him.

With a shock, the guard realized that he hadn't seen Stark in some time. "He was there a moment ago," he said, nervously.

"Go look for him," the warlord growled.

The guard rushed down the hall to the laboratory door and opened the viewing slat. Inside, Yinsen continued to work furiously. Stark was still nowhere in sight.

"Yinsen!" he called. "Yinsen!"

But Yinsen didn't turn away from his work. The guard realized Yinsen and Stark were up to something.

He fumbled with the keys, unlocked the door, and pulled it open.

As he did, an explosion rocked the hallway, blasting him back against the wall and knocking him unconscious.

Yinsen waved the smoke from the explosion away from his face. "Oh my goodness," he said. "That worked, all right."

Tony knew they had very little time before the warlord and his guards would reach the cell.

"Initialize the power sequence," he told Yinsen. Tony told him which keys to press on the battered laptop and Yinsen started up the computer program Tony had written.

Yinsen fumbled with the last few bolts on Tony's suit, then turned back to check on the computer's progress. The bars continued to move very slowly. He could hear the guards outside.

"We need more time," Yinsen whispered, with awful realization.

"Get to your cover," Tony said, his voice echoing inside the metal suit. "Remember the checkpoints — make sure each one is clear before you follow me out."

Yinsen turned to face him. "I'm going to buy you some time," he said, determinedly.

"No!" Tony cried. "Stick to the plan!"

But Yinsen ignored him. He turned and ran into the hallway, scooping up the guard's weapon from the floor.

"Yinsen!" Tony called.

But it was too late. Yinsen ran into the hall, firing the machine gun, trying to keep the guards back.

"Yinsen!" Tony called again, but his friend didn't reply.

Tony looked at the program bars on the laptop, but they were still moving so slowly. Gunfire sounded in the corridor outside. He could hear men running towards the lab.

Now! He needed the programs to finish now!

Suddenly, power surged and the lights dimmed into darkness. Two guards rushed in, firing. Tony grabbed them with his armoured hands and threw them aside. He paused for a moment and flexed his fingers.

He was huge and bulky, like a walking tank. Crude, grey metal armour covered him from head to toe. The repulsor-technology Arc generator glowed softly in his chest plate. He was a man of iron.

As more guards raced into the hall beyond the lab, Iron Man crashed through the doorway.

CHAPTER 7

The guards in the hall fired their weapons. Iron Man surged forward, bullets ricocheting off his armour. His heavy feet pounded the floor, shaking dust from the tunnel ceiling.

Seeing that their bullets had no effect, the guards jumped on him, trying to drag him down. Iron Man tossed them aside: the powerful motors in his armour gave him great strength.

Through the faceplate of his visor, Tony saw — in the distance — light from the cave exit. He lumbered forward, knocking guards out of his way as he went. An insurgent jumped out of a side passage and fired at point-blank range. Iron Man's armour dented, but the bullets still bounced off. He batted the guard aside.

More guards appeared before him, and then more still. Iron Man kept moving, picking up speed like a freight train. He plowed through the enemy, knocking them down like tenpins.

The constant hail of bullets was taking its toll, though. Tony felt the armour bending and weakening around him. Smoke rose from the suit's seams and Tony knew he needed to escape before it sustained more damage.

The tunnel opened up into a wide cavern, the main chamber of the complex. Yinsen lay crumpled on the ground near the exit, wounded.

"Look out!" Yinsen cried.

Iron Man turned just in time. A rocket-propelled grenade whizzed past his shoulder and exploded against the wall behind him. The wall crumbled and clouds of dust and smoke filled the room.

Through the debris, Tony spotted the warlord, holding the grenade launcher. The warlord smiled and calmly loaded another grenade. Iron Man whirled on him, activating the flamethrowers that were built into his armour.

The warlord screamed and ducked for cover, dropping the launcher. The weapon exploded as the flames hit it, and part of the tunnel collapsed around him.

Iron Man thumped across the room and knelt awkwardly at his friend's side. Yinsen's wounds looked very bad. Tony lifted his faceplate.

"Come on," Tony said, encouragingly. "We've got to go. Move for me. We've got a plan and we're going to stick to it."

"This was always the plan," Yinsen replied, weakly.

"Come on," said Tony. He refused to give up. "You've got to go and see your family."

A weak smile cracked Yinsen's blackened face. "My family is dead. I'm going to see them now, Stark," he said. "It's OK. I want this."

Tony understood. Yinsen wanted to join his family. He looked at his friend and smiled. "Thank you for saving me."

"Don't waste it," Yinsen whispered, meaningfully, "Don't waste your life."

He looked at Tony, then his eyes closed, and he slumped to the floor.

Rage filled Tony as he rose to his feet. He screamed as he barrelled down the tunnel and out the side of the mountain. As he emerged, the warlord's men kept firing, denting and tearing tiny pieces off Tony's armour.

Iron Man surged forward, heading for the ammunition dump.

A maze of boxes, all packed to the brim with weaponry, filled the valley.

Iron Man thundered into the maze. The boxes towered around him – enough armaments to start a war. Tony's eyes stung as he saw the Stark Industries logo emblazoned on the weapon crates. He fired his flamethrowers and the boxes exploded in flames.

The men followed him in, shooting as they came. The bullets ripped into Iron Man's armour. One caught on a seam and slammed into Tony's shoulder, knocking him off his feet.

His armour moved slowly and the joints ground together as Iron Man rose. Weapon crates burned all around now, but the men didn't seem to care; they wanted to bring Iron Man down for good.

Tony knew the suit couldn't take much more.

He fired one last flame at the weapon crates, then opened a metal flap on the armour's right arm. He flipped the switch inside and a screeching jet-engine-like whir filled the maze. The remaining guards covered their ears and fled.

Tony blasted off, soaring into the air like a rocket. As he went, the ammo dump began to explode – first one crate, then another, and then another, until the whole thing went up in flames.

Sweating, battered, and bruised, Tony concentrated on flying. He shot through the sky like a human cannonball. The desert streaked past below him, the scenery becoming a blur of speed and motion.

Then, suddenly, his jet boots gave out.

Tony plunged towards the sand, trying desperately to control his flight, but it was no use. He hit hard, spinning and rolling as he plowed into the sand. Pieces of his armour shredded off as he went. Finally, he skidded to a halt. The Iron Man armour was heavy against his skin.

He looked at his chest plate. The Arc generator glowed very faintly.

If he used much more of its energy, his heart would stop. Tony cut the power to the suit and slowly, painfully, dragged himself out of the shredded armour.

He had to keep moving. The warlord would be after him.

He staggered to his feet, leaving the shredded armour behind, and limped across the desert, away from the camp. His shoulder ached where the bullet had hit him. He clutched the wound, trying to stop the bleeding.

Don't pass out, he told himself. *Don't pass out.*

He kept walking for as long as he could. But soon he couldn't go any further. He hadn't eaten, or slept, or had any water since leaving the camp.

"Should have thought of bringing supplies," he told himself as the sun beat down on him.

He closed his eyes to try to block out the glare, but his eyelids didn't want to open again. Something pounded in his ears.

High above him he spotted a helicopter. The sound was very close, almost on top of him. He tried to run, but his legs wouldn't move.

He couldn't believe it. It was a US Army helicopter!

"Hey!" Tony screamed, waving his arms wildly. He slumped to the ground in utter relief.

The helicopter lowered itself onto the sand and a familiar figure ran out towards him.

"How was the 'Fun-vee'?" said Rhodey, bending down next to him.

Tony smiled, exhausted.

"Next time you ride with me, OK?" Rhodey said, putting his arm around his friend.

CHAPTER 8

Days later, the Air Force C-17 transport carrying Tony back to the United States touched down on the runway at Edwards Air Force Base. Tony, who was seated in a wheelchair, waited beside Rhodey as the plane's rear ramp descended.

As Rhodey wheeled his friend off the plane, Tony spotted Pepper standing on the tarmac. He struggled to his feet and Rhodey steadied him. Together they walked to where Pepper waited, beside Tony's limousine.

Two men approached them with a stretcher.

"What, are you kidding me with this?" Tony said.

Rhodey waved the men away.

Tony walked towards Pepper, who stood smiling uncontrollably. He didn't need to see the sympathy on her face to know how bad he looked. He was not the same man he'd been before the warlord captured him – he would never be.

"Your eyes are red," Tony said to her. "A few tears for your long-lost boss?"

"Tears of joy," she replied. "I hate job hunting."

Pepper helped Tony into the limo and then climbed in herself.

"Where to, sir?" Tony's chauffeur asked, hopping behind the wheel.

"Take us to the hospital, please, Happy," Pepper said.

"No," Tony replied. "I've been in captivity for three months. There are two things I want to do. I want an American cheeseburger. And I want to hold a press conference."

Pepper tried to argue, but Tony was immoveable.

"Hogan, drive," he told Happy. "Cheeseburger first."

A huge group of employees, including Obadiah Stane, had gathered outside the main office tower at the campus headquarters of Stark Industries. They burst into applause as Tony's limo pulled up.

Pepper looked at her boss, worried, and helped him get out of the car.

Stane stepped forward and embraced Tony in a bear hug.

"Tony, look at you!" he said. Then, more quietly, so only Tony and Pepper could hear, he added, "I thought we were meeting at the hospital."

Tony leaned on Stane's shoulder, and the two of them walked into the building's main entrance, followed by Pepper. Reporters packed the lobby from wall to wall.

Pepper didn't notice the man in the dark, tailored suit until he walked up behind her. He was around forty, with a stern face and impeccably groomed hair.

"Ms Potts, may I speak to you for a moment?" he asked.

"Oh, I'm not part of the press conference, but it's about to begin right now," she explained.

"I'm not a reporter," the man replied. "I'm Agent Phil Coulson, with the Strategic Homeland Intervention, Enforcement and Logistics Division."

"That's quite a mouthful," Pepper said, her eyes not leaving Tony for a moment.

35

"I know," Coulson said, handing her his business card. "We're working on it."

Pepper barely glanced at it. "Look, Mr Coulson," she said, "we've already spoken with the D.O.D., the FBI, the CIA, the —"

"We're a separate division with a more . . . specific focus," Coulson said. "We need to debrief Mr Stark about the circumstances of his escape."

"I'll put something in the book, shall I?" Pepper said, cutting him off.

"Thank you," Coulson said, nodding and walking away.

Obadiah Stane stepped up to the podium.

"Well, let's get this started . . ." he began, looking around for Tony.

But Tony had sat down at the foot of the podium and was unwrapping his second cheeseburger.

"Hey, would it be alright if everyone just sat down? It's a little less formal," said Tony, gesturing for the press to follow his lead and sit on the floor.

The gathered reporters looked at each other, confused, before lowering themselves to Tony's level.

"What's up with the love-in?" Rhodey whispered to Pepper.

"Don't look at me," she said, very amused, "I don't know what he's up to."

"I never got to say goodbye to my father," Tony began seriously, setting his burger aside. "There's questions I would have asked him . . . how he felt about what this company did, if he was conflicted, if he ever had doubts."

Tony paused and looked out over the crowd.

"I saw young Americans killed by the very weapons I created to

36

defend and protect them," he said, seriously.

Silence.

Finally, one of the reporters spoke up. "What happened over there?" he asked.

Tony looked thoughtful for a moment, and then all his emotions seemed to overflow. He stood up and stepped behind the podium.

"I had my eyes opened. I came to realize that I have more to offer this world than just making things to blow up. And that is why, effective immediately, I am shutting down the weapons manufacture division of Stark International —"

Pepper's jaw dropped. The rest of the room erupted into chaos. Stane moved to cut him off.

Tony ploughed on, ". . . until such a time as I can decide what the future of this company will be, what direction it should take — one that I'm comfortable with and that is consistent with the highest good for this country, as well."

Reporters shouted questions as Tony stepped back and Stane took the podium.

"OK," Stane said. "What we should take away from this is that Tony's back! He's healthier than ever, we're going to have a little internal discussion and we'll get back to you."

Stane found Tony inside the Arc Reactor building.

"That went well," Stane said, sarcastically.

"Did I just paint a target on the back of my head?" Tony asked.

"Your head?" Stane replied. "What about my head? How much do you think our stock is going to drop tomorrow?"

Tony thought a moment. "Optimistically: forty points."

"Minimum," Stane said. "Tony, we are a weapons manufacturer."

"I don't want a body count to be our only legacy," Tony said.

Stane frowned at him. "What we do here keeps the world from falling into chaos."

"Not based on what I saw," Tony said. "We're not doing a good enough job. We can do better. We're going to do something else."

"Like what?" Stane asked. "You want us to make baby bottles?"

"I think we should take another look into Arc Reactor technology," Tony mused.

"The Arc Reactor was a publicity stunt," Stane said. "We built it to shut up the hippies."

"It works," said Tony.

"Yeah, as a science project," Stane replied. "It was never cost-effective. We knew that before we built it. Arc Reactor technology is a dead end. Right?"

"Maybe," Tony replied.

Stane looked at him anxiously. "There haven't been any breakthroughs in thirty years. Right?"

Tony shook his head. "Could you have a lousier poker face? Just tell me, who told you? Pepper? Rhodey?"

"Come on," Stane said. "I want to see it."

"Was it Rhodey?" Tony asked.

"Just show it to me," Stane said.

Tony ripped open his shirt, revealing the glowing electronic unit in the middle of his chest.

"Well," Stane said, marvelling. He took a very deep breath and continued. "Listen, we're a team. There's nothing we can't do if we stick together, like your father and I. No more of this ready-fire-aim business."

Stane straightened up. "You've got to let me handle this. I want you to promise me that you're going to lay low."

But 'laying low' had never been something Tony Stark was good at.

CHAPTER 9

Pepper was perched nervously on the edge of the sofa in Tony's plush living room. A finance advice show blared news about Stark International.

"I have one recommendation," the moderator was saying. "Sell! Abandon ship."

Behind him, the day's newspaper headlines blazed across the screen — 'Stark Raving Mad?', 'Stark Lunacy', and other similar rants.

When Tony's voice came over the intercom, Pepper jumped. "Pepper, how big are your hands?" he asked.

She looked confused.

"Get down here, I need you," he said.

Frowning, she hurried through the security doors and down to Tony's lab. When she arrived, she found the workshop dimly lit, dirty and disorganized. Tony was sitting in a chair, shirtless, his chest plate glowing slightly.

Pepper steeled herself. Though she knew the device implanted in his chest had saved Tony's life, she still wasn't used to it.

"I just need your help for a sec," Tony said.

She stared at the glowing repulsor-tech device.

"Is that the thing that's keeping you alive?" she asked, awestruck.

"It *was*," he replied. "It's now an antique. This is what will be keeping me alive for the foreseeable future." He held up a similar device that looked much more high-tech and powerful. "I'm swapping it out for an upgraded unit and I just ran into a little speed bump," Tony said.

"Speed bump? What does that mean?" Pepper asked.

"Just a little snag," Tony said, casually. "There's an exposed wire under this device . . ." as he talked, he turned the Arc Reactor in his chest until it clicked, then removed it. He handed it to Pepper to discard.

"I just want you to reach in and gently lift the wire out," he told her, pointing at the hole in his chest.

"Is it safe?" she gasped, terrified.

"Yeah," he assured her. "Just don't let it touch the socket wall."

Pepper's stomach turned as she gingerly reached her hand into the socket. She managed to pull out the offending wire, but also yanked out the electromagnet at the end of it, by accident.

"I was not expecting that," said Tony, as the heart monitor behind him went into overdrive.

"What?" shrieked Pepper. "What did I do? What's wrong?"

"Oh nothing, I'm just going into cardiac arrest," Tony replied, very calmly.

Pepper's stomach twisted into a knot. "I thought you said it was safe!"

"We've got to hurry," Tony replied.

Pepper felt the blood drain from her face.

"Take this," Tony said, handing her the new chest piece. "We've got to switch it over real quick."

He kept talking, giving quick but complete directions so she could replace the unit.

Somehow, Pepper managed to get through the procedure without passing out.

"Are you OK?" she said, breathlessly, when it was done.

"Yeah, I feel great," he replied, laughing. "Are you OK?"

She glared at him. "Don't ever, ever, ever, ask me to do anything like that ever again!"

"I don't have anyone but you," Tony replied, seriously.

He looked into her eyes and, for a moment, she felt something for him she'd never felt before. There was a pause, then they both turned away.

Pepper picked up the old unit. "What should I do with this?" she asked. The tiny power plant glowed slightly in her hand.

"Destroy it," Tony replied, simply. "Incinerate it."

Pepper frowned and looked sentimentally at the glowing 'heart'. "You don't want to keep it?"

"Pepper," Tony said, "I have been called many things, but 'nostalgic' is not one of them."

Pepper straightened up. "Will that be all, Mr Stark?"

"That will be all, Ms Potts."

She left the room. Tony smiled.

In a hangar at Edwards Air Force Base, Rhodey was striding across the floor, delivering a speech to a team of eager recruits.

"The future of air combat – is it manned or unmanned? In my experience, no unmanned aerial vehicle will ever trump a pilot's instinct, his insight, or his judgement."

"Colonel," interrupted Tony, emerging from behind an aircraft. "Why not a pilot without the plane?"

Rhodey smiled and dismissed the pilots so he could speak to Tony privately.

"I'm surprised!" he marvelled. "I didn't expect to see you walking around so soon."

"I'm doing a little better than walking," Tony replied, excitedly. "Rhodey, I'm working on something big — I want you to be part of it."

Rhodey looked relieved. "You're about to make a whole lot of people really happy, because that little stunt at the press conference — that was a doozy."

'Yeah," Tony said, awkwardly. "This is not for the military. It's . . . different."

Rhodey frowned. Tony was still set on giving up weapons, by the sound of it. "What, you're a humanitarian now, or something?"

"I need you to listen to me —" Tony pleaded.

"No!" shouted Rhodey, angrily. "What you need is time to get your head right. I'm serious." He paused. "It's nice seeing you, Tony."

"Thanks," said Tony quietly, as Rhodey walked away. He was going to have to go it alone.

Tony went straight back to his workshop and fired up his sophisticated computer system. He ran his fingers over the touch-screen key-pad.

"Jarvis, you up?" he asked the computer.

"For you, sir, always," replied Jarvis's almost-human voice.

"I'd like to open a new project file. Index as 'Mark II'."

Tony brought up a diagram of the Iron Man suit on the screen and transferred it to a holographic plate in the centre of the room. The suit hovered above the plate in 3-D.

"Shall I store this on the Stark Industires central database?" Jarvis asked.

"I don't know who to trust right now," replied Tony, walking over to the hologram. "Until further notice, why don't we just keep everything on my private server."

"Working on a secret project, are we, sir?" asked Jarvis.

Tony stared at the Iron Man suit, then started manipulating the hologram, removing parts of the armour he wanted to redesign.

"I don't want this winding up in the wrong hands," he said.

Half a world away, in the deserts of Afghanistan, a swarm of ragged men scoured the sand dunes, looking for items to scavenge. Men were putting pieces they had found into the back of a corroded pickup truck.

"Over here! I found something!" one man called, pointing to a battered piece of metal protruding from the sand. He tugged the metal free and held it high, as though it were a trophy. It was Tony's old Iron Man mask.

A powerful man turned to look. It was the warlord. He walked over to look at the discovery. The man handed it to him, smiling up at the warlord's scarred and burned face, hoping for approval.

The warlord merely nodded, held the mask aloft, and stared into its empty eye sockets.

CHAPTER 10

Sketches and designs lay scattered across the worktable in Tony's lab as he tinkered with his newest invention – a pair of shining metal boots.

When he'd finished his adjustments, Tony put on the boots and stepped into a test area in the middle of the lab floor. He draped a bandolier-like control device around his shoulders and hooked it all into his chest unit.

"OK, let's do this right. Starting mark half a metre back and centre," said Tony, as he positioned himself. Jarvis focused a camera on Tony, ready to record his experiment.

"Look alive, you're on standby for fire safety," Tony instructed a robot behind him.

"Activate hand controls," Tony said, gripping the bandolier's joystick controls. "We'll start off nice and easy," he said. "Ten per cent thrust capacity." He pressed the activators on the joysticks.

Instantly, the boot jets fired and he shot upwards, smacking straight into the concrete ceiling of his workshop and crashing down into a pile of cardboard boxes in the corner. The robot sprayed a jet of fire extinguisher on top of him.

Days later, Pepper came into the workshop as Tony fiddled with a pair of metal gauntlets.

"Obadiah's upstairs," she said. "Should I tell him you're in?"

Tony put on one of the gloves and Pepper frowned. "I thought you said you were done making weapons?"

"It's not a weapon," Tony replied. "It's a flight stabilizer."

He pointed the glove across the lab and activated the repulsor-technology pads in the palms. A blast of light issued forth from his hands. It hit a toolbox 15 feet away, knocking it over and scattering the wrenches inside across the floor. Pepper jumped in fright.

"I didn't expect that," Tony said, with a sheepish grin.

Tony reached the living room just as Obadiah Stane set a pizza down on the coffee table. Stane flashed the billionaire a concerned smile.

"Oh wow, it went bad, huh?" asked Tony.

"Just because I brought pizza back from New York, doesn't mean it went bad," said Obadiah. "But it would have gone better if you were there."

Tony bit into a slice of pizza. "You told me to lay low," he shrugged. "That's what I've been doing. And you take care of all the —"

"Oh come on," interrupted Obadiah, "in public, yes. This was a board of directors meeting."

"This was . . . what?" said Tony, utterly shocked.

Obadiah sat down next to him and took a deep breath.

"The board is claiming post-traumatic stress. They're filing an injunction against you. They want to lock you out."

Tony's jaw dropped. "What? Because the stock dipped forty points? We knew that was going to happen."

"Fifty-six and a half," Pepper piped up.

"It doesn't matter!" Tony said, angrily. "We own the controlling

46

interest in the company."

Obadiah hung his head. "Tony, the board has rights, too. They're making the case that you — and your new 'direction' — isn't in the company's best interests."

"I'm being responsible! That's my new 'direction'. This is great," he said, throwing up his hands and storming towards the door.

"Tony!" Stane said, jumping up and following him. He put his hand reassuringly on Tony's shoulder. "Listen, I'm trying to turn this thing around. But you've got to give me something — something to pitch them." He pointed at the RT in Tony's chest. "Let me have the engineers anaylze that, draw up some specs —"

"No," Tony replied, firmly. "Absolutely not. This one stays with me."

He ran down the stairs, towards his workshop.

"You mind if I come down there and see what you're doing?" asked Obadiah, shouting after him.

"Good night, Obi," called Tony, as he disappeared into his private lab.

It took him a few more days to hook the boot units, the control bandolier, and the new gauntlets together. Once he'd done it, though, he couldn't resist trying out the setup.

Tony positioned himself in the test area again.

"Day eleven, test thirty-seven, configuration 2.0. For lack of a better option, you're still on fire safety," he said, pointing at the robot who'd extinguished him unneccesarily the last time.

"Alright, nice and easy. Seriously, just going to start off with 1 per cent thrust capacity. In three, two, one . . ."

He activated the boot jets and manipulated the controls.

Slowly, he rose off the floor and hovered in the air. The repulsor stabilizers in the gloves kicked in, steadying his flight. He moved up in the air, holding his arms out like a tightrope walker. Looking satisifed, he lowered himself to the ground again.

"Again," he instructed Jarvis, "let's bring it up to 2.5!"

Tony rose into the air again and, after gaining his balance, he floated slowly around the room, dodging expensive pieces of electronic equipment and avoiding the cars, workbench and other obstacles.

He nearly bumped his head on the ceiling twice and came perilously close to the roof of his Porsche, but he didn't hit anything. His papers and a few light objects scattered out of his way as he flew, repelled by the repulsor forces powering the boots and the gauntlets.

He cut the propulsion, landed softly near his workbench, and grinned at one of Jarvis's sensors.

"Yeah," Tony said. "I can fly."

CHAPTER 11

Tony's metal boots clanked across the workshop floor. The armour felt heavy, so he made an adjustment to the servo-motors that powered it. His repulsor-technology heart glowed more brightly within his chest plate, and the suit moved more easily.

He flexed his arms and the suit flexed with him. The ailerons, air brakes and other flying controls popped out on command, just as they were supposed to. The new armour covering him from head-to-toe felt good.

He pressed a button on a lab console and downloaded Jarvis's program into the suit's computer system. The armour's heads-up display flashed to life.

"Jarvis, are you there?" he asked.

"At your service, sir," the computerized butler replied.

Tony instructed the computer to run a series of virtual tests. The multi-layered metal flaps on the suit bristled and clicked.

"Test complete," announced Jarvis. "Preparing to power down and begin diagnostics."

But Tony had other ideas. "Yeah, tell you what, do a weather and ATC check, start focusing in on ground control." A map of the local terrain appeared on his heads-up display, complete with the flight paths of aeroplanes in the area.

"There are terabytes of calculations still needed before an actual

49

flight," Jarvis warned.

Behind his metal helmet, Tony smiled. "Jarvis, sometimes you've got to run before you can walk."

Tony fired up the boots and the gauntlet repulsors. He rose into the air and slowly hovered out of the workshop's garage doors and along the driveway. He kicked up the power and blasted into the night sky.

"Woo-hoo!" he yelled in excitement.

Iron Man weaved and wobbled through the air, trying to keep the horizon steady. He tried poses he'd seen in various movies, books and comics about flying superheroes, but each one seemed more unstable than the previous one.

Then he had an idea. You're jet powered, he told himself. Think like a jet.

He thrust his chest out, held his chin up, kept his knees and feet together, and flung his arms out to the side — like a delta-winged fighter aircraft.

To his delight, the pose worked, and he zoomed through the air like a human missile. He pulled a few exhilarating banked turns, and then followed the ribbon of the Pacific Coast Highway south to Santa Monica. Onlookers gaped in awe as Iron Man buzzed the giant Ferris wheel on the pier.

Tony smiled and arced upwards in a power climb. The clouds streaked past like misty dreams and soon he emerged into a perfect, starry night.

"OK, let's see what this thing can do!" Tony said. "What's the SR-71's record?"

A diagnostic of the famous SR-71 reconnaisance jet flashed onto his display.

"The altitude record for fixed-wing flight is 82,000 feet, sir," answered Jarvis.

"Records were made to be broken," Tony replied, zooming even higher into the sky.

He was so high up now that the world seemed a tiny, distant place. Ice crystals formed on the inside of his helmet.

"Sir, there is a potentially fatal build-up of ice occurring," warned Jarvis.

Caught up in the moment, Tony didn't listen. Instead, he zoomed ever higher, chasing the stars. The moon beckoned before him, huge and impossibly bright. Tony didn't ever remember seeing anything more beautiful in his life.

Suddenly, the heads-up display inside Tony's helmet went dark. Iron Man's thrusters sputtered and died. The suit felt heavy and awkward. Tony glanced at his chest plate – it wasn't glowing.

The weight of the armour overcame his momentum and he plummeted, pinwheeling towards the earth.

"Uh, Jarvis?" Tony called. "Jarvis!" The earth zoomed up towards him.

"Come on, we've got to break the ice!" Tony yelled to the silent computer system.

He plummeted through the clouds. The coastline appeared below, the lights of the city blazed into view, and the snaking curve of the highway revealed itself.

Grasping desperately at his leg, Tony managed to reach a dial in the armour. He turned it and the metal plates all over his body flipped outwards, cracking the layer of ice on top.

Suddenly, the heads-up display flickered back to life. Power surged through the suit's servo-motors and circuits.

Tony fought to bring the armour back under control. He righted himself and flew back towards the mansion. He aimed for the driveway, struggling to maintain stability. He regained control and hovered steadily over the drive, ready for a gentle landing.

"Kill power," Tony said, proudly.

An accidental shift of his weight sent him crashing through the roof of the mansion.

Shattered beams and plaster rained around him as he broke through the ceiling of his garage and landed on top of his Shelby Cobra.

The impact shook his entire body and set off every car alarm in the garage. And to top it all off, the fire robot doused him again.

After Tony had climbed out of his armour and applied a big bag of ice to the growing bump on his head, he felt a little dejected. There was still a lot of work to do on the suit. He walked through his workshop, kicking boxes out of his path in frustration.

Suddenly, he caught sight of something sitting on the edge of his worktable. A note on the top said, 'From Pepper'. Intrigued, Tony ripped the package open.

Inside was his old chest device, encased in Lucite. The Reactor glowed faintly inside the clear plastic. Tony knew it would continue to glow for years. The casing had an inscription: PROOF THAT TONY STARK HAS A HEART. Tony smiled to himself.

Half a world away, the warlord of the Ten Rings stared at the grey suit of armour being assembled on the lab table in his new hideout.

"Amazing," he muttered. Amazing that something like this could nearly destroy his whole operation.

It would be difficult to complete the reassembly without either Yinsen or Stark to guide his workers, but he knew the job would eventually get done.

And then he would own a weapon that would be the envy of even the largest corporations and governments.

The warlord smiled and, for once, he did not mind the stiffness of his scarred face.

Back in Tony's lab, the inventor was reinspired and hard at work, typing design notes into his computer. Graphics and data scrolled down the lab's many monitors.

"Notes: main transducer felt sluggish at plus forty altitude. Hull pressurization is problematic. I think the icing is a probable factor."

"A very astute observation, sir," Jarvis said, sarcastically. "Perhaps if you intend to visit other planets, we should improve the exosystems."

"Reconfigure the suit using the gold-titanium alloy from the Seraphim Tactical Satellite. It should ensure fuselage integrity, while maintaining power-to-weight ratio."

"Shall I render using proposed specifications on screen?" Jarvis asked.

"Thrill me."

On-screen, the sleek form of the Mark II armour transformed into an even sleeker, golden Mark III prototype.

Tony regarded it and rubbed his chin. "A little . . . ostentatious, don't you think?"

"What was I thinking? You're usually so discreet," responded Jarvis.

Tony glanced over at his collection of cars and motorcycles, seeking inspiration in their paint jobs.

53

"Throw a little hot-rod red in there," he said, pointing to the screen.

"Yes," mused Jarivs, "that should help you keep a low profile."

The computer graphics prototype changed colour appropriately.

Just then, Tony noticed the image on the television, which had been playing silently in the background. He turned up the volume.

A local reporter stood outside a grand entertainment hall where a huge crowd was gathering. "Tonight's red-hot red carpet is right here at the Walt Disney Concert Hall, where Tony Stark's annual benefit for the Firefighter Family Fund has become *the* place to be for LA's high-society."

Tony looked confused. He vaguely remembered Pepper mentioning it to him.

"But this great cause is only part of the story," the reporter continued. "The man who hosts the event hasn't been seen in public since his bizarre and highly controversial press conference. Some claim he is suffering from post-traumatic stress and has been bed-ridden for weeks. Whatever the case may be, no one expects an appearance from him tonight."

Tony scoffed and returned his attention to the design screen. The red-and-gold Iron Man Mark III uniform looked good — very good.

"I like it," Tony decided. "Paint it."

"Commencing automated assembly. Estimated completion time is five hours," Jarvis noted. Nearby, the lab's automated tooling and manufacturing machines sprang to life.

"Good," Tony said. "Don't wait up for me, honey." He set his watch and headed out of the door.

CHAPTER 12

The crowd outside the concert hall filled the entire avenue and overflowed into the surrounding streets. The concert-goers were a mix of celebrities, generals, business tycoons and movie stars.

Flashbulbs lit the scene as Tony pulled his sports car up to the curb. The crowd roared as Tony stepped onto the red carpet.

He sauntered over to where Obadiah Stane stood, giving interviews about the future of Stark Industries.

"What's the world coming to, when a guy's got to crash his own party?" joked Tony — but there was an edge to his voice.

"Look at you! Hey, what a surprise," Stane laughed, looking nervous.

Tony shrugged. "I'll see you inside."

"Listen, just take it slow, OK?" Stane said. "I've got the board right where we want them." He nodded towards a group of Stark International executives milling around with the red carpet crowd.

"You got it," Tony replied, heading for the theatre doors, anxious not to get caught up in company business.

The interior of the venue was almost as crowded as outside. Music filled the concert hall as happy couples whirled around the dance floor. Tony headed for the bar and was immediately approached by a serious-looking man.

"Mr Stark? Agent Coulson."

"Oh yeah," said Tony. The guy from the, the —"

"Strategic Homeland Intervention, Enforcement and Logistics Division," the agent offered.

"Gotta get a new name for that," said Tony, looking out distractedly across the dancefloor.

"Yeah, I hear that a lot," the agent replied. "Listen, I know this must be a trying time for you, but we need to debrief you. There's still a lot of unanswered questions and time can be a factor with these things. Let's just put something in the book. How about the 24th, 7pm at Stark Industries?"

Just then, Tony spotted Pepper standing on the dancefloor. She looked stunning in a blue silk evening gown. Tony's jaw dropped and he was no longer listening to Agent Coulson.

"Tell you what," he said to Coulson, not taking his eyes from Pepper, "you got it. I'm going to go and speak to my assistant and we can make a date."

Tony made a beeline for her. She looked surprised and pleased to see him.

"You look fantastic," Tony said, "I didn't recognize you. Where did you get that dress?"

"Thanks," she said, smiling. "It was a birthday present — from you, actually."

"I have great taste," Tony said. "Want to dance?" He took her hand and whisked her onto the dance floor. She looked away from him bashfully.

"Am I making you uncomfortable?" Tony said.

"Er, no," she replied, her face slightly flushed. "I always forget to wear deodorant and dance with my boss in front of everyone I work with, in a dress with no back."

"I could fire you, if that would take the edge off," Tony suggested.

She grinned. "I don't think you could tie your shoes without me."

"I'd make it," Tony said.

"What's your Social Security number?" she asked.

"Uh . . ." Tony began.

She laughed.

Tony couldn't stop staring at her. Pepper looked down, embarrassed.

"How about a little air?" he suggested.

"Yes, I need some air," Pepper replied, instantly.

They retired to the veranda outside to catch their breaths. Pepper looked beautiful in the starlight. They stood silently for a moment.

"Can I get you something to drink?" Tony finally asked.

"Yes, please," she said.

Tony left and picked up two drinks from the buffet table. Before he could return to Pepper, though, reporter Christine Everhart strode up to him. She had a folder under her arm.

"Mr Stark," she said, shoving a microphone into his face, "I was hoping I could get a reaction from you on your company's involvement in this latest atrocity."

"Hey, they just put my name on the invitation, I don't know what to tell you," Tony explained, loosening his collar.

She opened the folder and thrust it towards him. Inside, there were pictures of Ten Rings separatists clutching Stark machine guns and other weapons. Behind them, a village burned.

Tony looked at the photos in horror. "When were these taken?" he asked.

"Yesterday," she replied.

"I didn't approve any shipment," Tony said. He felt as though the world was crumbling around him.

"Well, your company did," Christine replied.

"Well, I'm not my company," said Tony, firmly.

Tony raced outside to find Obadiah.

"Have you seen these pictures?" he asked him, aghast.

Obadiah grabbed Tony's elbow and hustled him away from the reporters. "Tony, Tony," he said calmly. "You can't afford to be this naïve."

"Naïve?" Tony said. "Are we double-dealing under the table?"

They stared at each other.

"Let's take a picture, come on," said Stane, putting his arm around Tony and turning him towards the waiting cameras. Stane smiled as flash bulbs popped all around them.

"Tony," he whispered, "who do you think locked you out? I was the one who filed the injunction against you."

Tony couldn't believe it. Betrayed by his father's oldest friend. He stared straight ahead in shock.

"It was the only way I could protect you," added Stane, as he walked away and climbed into his waiting limousine.

CHAPTER 13

Tony sat hunched over his workbench, wearing a prototype of the Mark III Iron Man gauntlet. On the wall in front of him, a large flat-screen TV monitor blared with the latest news.

The TV showed long lines of refugees streaming out of the ruins of Gulmira. "Simple farmers and herders from peaceful villages have been driven from their homes, displaced from their lands by warlords, emboldened by a new-found power," the reporter said.

Tony watched as the scene on the TV switched, now showing triumphant Ten Rings separatists running rampant through Gulmira City.

"Recent violence has been attributed to a group of foreign fighters, referred to by locals as the 'Ten Rings'," continued the reporter. "As you can see, these men are heavily armed and on a mission that could prove fatal to anyone who stands in their way." The TV showed the men armed with machine guns, missiles and other sophisticated weapons. Stark weapons.

Tony aimed the gauntlet at a hanging light fixture 20 feet away and activated the repulsor unit. The lights sparked and fizzled and fell from the ceiling.

As the TV continued to show weeping, homeless refugees, Tony adjusted the gauntlet, raising the power level. He pointed it towards a window on the far side of the lab and fired. The blast shattered the glass and knocked a nearby picture off the wall.

"With no international political will or pressure," the TV reporter concluded, "there is very little hope for these refugees – refugees who can only wonder: who, if anyone, will help?"

Tony made a final adjustment to the gauntlet and blasted two other windows. As silence descended over the lab, he nodded in satisfaction.

It took him a few minutes to suit up in his new armour. As the mask clasped shut over his face, Tony narrowed his eyes in grim determination. Powering up his jet boots, he streaked into the sky, setting his onboard navigation system for Gulmira.

Gunshots and explosions filled the air in Gulmira City. Ten Rings rebels ran riot among the hovels and refugee tents, dragging women and children into trucks and lining up the men for execution.

A small boy watched in horror as his father was pushed roughly against a wall. Breaking free from a rebel's grasp, the boy made a dash across the square, embracing his father and crying.

"What is this?" shouted one of the rebels, pulling the boy away.

"Papa!" screamed the boy, tears rolling down his face.

Suddenly, a roaring sound filled the air and the boy looked up to see a red and gold object barelling towards them through the air.

Iron Man dropped out of the sky, landing between the rebels and their intended victim. The rebels fired at Iron Man, but the bullets bounced off his improved armour without even making a dent. Tony powered up the repulsor units in his gloves. He fired, knocking out a dozen men and overturning their jeep with the first burst.

He turned to dispatch another group of rebels, but saw that they had each grabbed an innocent refugee, and were threatening to shoot if Tony tried to attack them. The men were standing so close to the captives, that if Tony had been armed with a normal gun, he would not have been able to aim accurately enough to pick off the bad guys from the good guys.

Luckily for Tony, he had a more precise weapon. His shoulder plates opened up to reveal a set of micro machine-guns and on Tony's heads-up display, a sophisticated targeting system pinpointed each rebel. He fired four shots at once and took out the men, leaving the civilians standing unharmed.

The boy ran to his father and hugged him.

Inside his helmet, Tony Stark smiled.

Iron Man lifted off, intent on another purpose. His heads-up display located a store of Jericho missiles and Tony's weapons system locked onto them, ready to fire.

Then, without warning, something struck him hard in the back and Iron Man plummeted to the ground, creating a huge crater with the impact. Unharmed, he lifted himself out of the hole in the ground and turned to face the tank that had shot at him.

It trained its turret cannon towards Iron Man as he rose to his feet.

Tony studied the tank's schematic on his heads-up display. The tank was Stark designed, and his computer files showed him everything about it, including its weaknesses.

The tank fired again, but Iron Man was already moving.

A mini-missile launcher popped open on Tony's left gauntlet. Iron Man fired the missile into the tank, hitting it between the body and turret. The tank's systems overloaded and, moments later, it exploded.

Tony took off again, heading for home, and exploding every Jericho missile he could locate in his wake.

Over in Edwards Air Force Base, Tony's antics were causing a ruckus. Senior airforce recruits observed the unidentified flying object on their surveillance monitors.

"What was that?" asked one in disbelief.

"I've got the CIA on the line," said another, "they want to know if it's us."

'No! It is defnitely not us," Major Allen said, observing the chaos. "It wasn't Navy, it wasn't Marines. I need answers! Get me Colonel Rhodes from Weapons y down here, now!" he ordered.

As Iron Man sped through the sky, Colonel Rhodes strode into the room.

"So this thing just appeared out of nowhere? How come it didn't show up on the radar?" he asked, trying to ascertain what the object might be.

"It's tiny, sir," answered one of the men. "We think it's an Unmanned Aerial Vehicle."

"What are we dealing with here?" Major Allen asked Colonel Rhodes.

Rhodey thought for a moment, frowned, and then said, "Let me make a call." He picked up his phone and punched in Tony Stark's private number. A moment later, Tony's voice came over the earpiece.

"Hello?"

Rhodey could barely hear him; it was a terrible connection. "Tony, it's Rhodes. What's that noise?"

"I'm driving with the top down," Tony replied.

"I need your help right now," Rhodey said, studying the ongoing satellite pictures. "We've got a weapons depot that was just blown up a few clicks from where you were being held captive."

"Well, that's a hot spot," said Tony. "Sounds like someone stepped in and did your job for you."

"Why do you sound out of breath, Tony?" asked Rhodey, suspiciously.

"I'm not, I was just jogging in the canyon," Tony replied.

"I thought you said you were driving," said Rhodey.

"Right, I was driving. To the canyon. Where I'm going to jog." Tony really needed to sign off soon – he couldn't lie very well at high altitude.

"You sure you don't have any tech in that area I should know about?" asked Rhodey, giving him one more chance to confess, if he was hiding something.

"Nope," Tony said.

"OK, good. Because I'm staring at one right now," Rhodey said, "and it's about to get blown to kingdom come."

Tony looked up as two US Air Force F-22 Raptors streaked out of the sky towards him.

"This is my exit," he said, lying to Rhodey. "I gotta go." He switched off the phone link inside his helmet.

The jets screamed ahead, gaining on him. Tony turned on the armour's turbo booster and shot forward. He pulled into a tight bank, but the planes remained on his tail.

Beads of sweat rolled down Tony's back. Every time he turned, the planes turned with him. But would they fire? He was on their side, after all.

Of course, they didn't know that.

"Control room, this is Whiplash One, I have the bogey in my sights," one of the pilots advised Rhodey over his radio.

"Whiplash One, what is it?" asked Rhodey.

"I have no idea," said the pilot, looking at the red and gold object speeding through the air.

"Do you have radio contact?" asked Major Allen.

"Non-responsive, sir," affirmed the pilot.

"Then you are clear to engage," ordered the Major.

Tony's heads-up display showed the jets' weapons systems trying to lock on. He knew it wouldn't be long before they had him in their sights. He powered up his supersonic drive and blasted away at top speed.

"The bogey just went supersonic, I've got a lock!" shouted the pilot.

Tony glanced back over his shoulder as the lead jet fired a missile at him.

CHAPTER 14

The missile streaked straight towards Iron Man. In his revamped armour, Tony was as fast as the jets – but the sidewinder missile was faster still. Tony concentrated, sending every iota of power he could into the suit's thrusters but, each moment, his heads-up display showed the missile gaining on him.

Jarvis's voice remained calm. "Inbound missile," he announced.

Tony activated the suit's counter measures. Instantly a hatch popped open, and big, confetti-like flakes of metal burst into the air. The sidewinder hit the chaff and exploded. The fireball from the explosion surrounded Iron Man, but Tony didn't even feel it through the armour.

Unfortunately, the F-22 jets hadn't given up yet.

Iron Man dived towards the ground, rolled to his left, banked right. The Raptors followed close behind. Tony flew as fast as he could, trying to keep the jets from locking on again. He banked into a hard turn. The G-force meter inside his helmet went from green to yellow to red. The world around him blurred, and Tony nearly blacked out.

The F-22s sprayed machine-gun fire into Iron Man's path. White-hot tracer rounds streaked past Tony, exploding and ricocheting off his armour. For the first time, the new suit buckled and tore.

Tony grimaced and said, "Deploy flaps!"

Instantly, tiny retro-rockets popped out of the armour and fired, slowing Iron Man to a halt in seconds. Tony grunted as G-forces pressed him against the inside of the suit.

The jets shot past Iron Man, twin blurs of aviation grey. Tony breathed a sigh of relief. The Raptors would be miles away before they could turn back on him again.

"That thing just dropped off the radar, sir," advised one of the men in the control room.

"No way that's a UAV," added one of the pilots.

Just then, Rhodey's mobile phone started ringing. The display showed that Tony was calling him. Rhodey shook his head.

"Hello?" Rhodey said.

"Hi Rhodey. What you were asking before — it's me," Tony replied.

Rhodey's voice came back hushed, as though he didn't want the people with him to overhear. "No, see, this isn't a game. You do not send civilian equipment into my active war zone, you understand that?"

"This is not a piece of equipment. I'm in it. It's me!" said Tony, urgently.

"Return to base," Major Allen ordered the planes, in the background.

But when Whiplash Two banked left, the wingman in the other jet spotted something on the underside of the craft. Iron Man was clamped onto it.

"On your belly!" Whiplash One called. "It looks like a — a man!"

Rhodey's mouth dropped open.

"What?" Whiplash Two asked, seemingly unable to believe it.

"Shake him off! Roll!" said the second pilot.

The F-22 Raptor immediately began a series of swoops, dives and turns. Even with his armour-enhanced fingers, Tony barely hung on. The manoeuvres shook him inside the suit like nails inside a tin can.

Iron Man lost his grip and tumbled through the air. He smashed into Whiplash One's tail fin, ripping it off. The jet careened towards the ground.

"I'm hit!" the pilot cried. He pushed the eject button and the canopy of his aircraft flew off. The rocket-powered cockpit chair zoomed clear of the crippled aircraft, but the chair's parachute failed to open.

"Whiplash One down," said a man in the control room.

"Whiplash Two, do you see a chute?" Major Allen called.

"Negative!" the pilot replied. "No chute! No chute!"

Iron Man streaked forward. The heads-up display gave Tony the information he needed. He rocketed towards the falling pilot.

"Sir, I've got a visual on the bogey," Whiplash Two said.

"Whiplash Two," Major Allen called, "re-engage. If you get a clear shot, you take it!"

"Major," Rhodey warned, "we don't even know what we're shooting at. Call off the Raptors."

"That thing just took out an F-22 in a legal no-fly zone," barked the Major. "Whiplash Two, if you have a clear shot, take it!" he ordered.

Inside Tony's helmet, Jarvis advised him of the situation. "You've been re-engaged. Execute evasive manoeuvre."

"Keep going!" Tony yelled in response.

He zoomed towards the falling pilot and, at the last instant, Iron Man's metal fingers found the jammed chute mechanism and ripped it open.

The pilot's chute deployed with a loud whooshing sound. The parachute caught the air and jerked the pilot upwards, away from Iron Man. The chute billowed out, gliding the pilot safely towards earth.

Beneath his helmet, Tony grinned.

"Good chute! Good chute!" Whiplash Two called.

The control room burst into applause.

Iron Man fired his thrusters, banking sharply, and barely avoided slamming into the ground. Whiplash Two dropped back and Tony streaked away to safety.

Rhodey picked up his phone. "Tony, you still there?"

"Hey, thanks," Tony replied.

"You're crazy!" Rhodey whispered. "You owe me a plane, you know that?"

"Yeah, well, technically he hit me," Tony laughed. "Now are you going to come by and see what I'm working on?"

"No, no, no," Rhodey said, smiling. "The less I know, the better."

CHAPTER 15

Pepper heard strange noises as she walked down the steps towards Tony's workshop. Machinery whirred and Tony was saying 'ouch' a lot.

As she turned the corner, she saw him standing on a platform, encased in red and gold armour, with articulated robot arms working around him to remove the pieces.

"What's going on here?" she said, amazed, as she walked towards him.

Tony hadn't realized he was being watched. He turned to look over his shoulder. "Let's face it," he said, deadpan, "this is not the worst thing you've caught me doing."

Pepper looked closer at the scarred and pitted armour. "Are those bullet holes?" she gasped.

A train of black SUVs wound through the desert towards the Ten Rings' hideout. The vehicles stopped near the warlord's tent, and private security guards stepped out. They took up defensive positions around the convoy.

Obadiah Stane stepped from his SUV as the warlord pulled back the tent flaps.

"Welcome," the warlord said. Seeing Stane's gaze linger on his scarred face, he added, "Compliments of Tony Stark."

"If you'd killed him when you were supposed to," Stane said, "you'd still have a face."

The warlord's smile turned into a savage grimace.

"You paid us trinkets to kill a prince," he said.

"Show me the weapon," Stane replied.

The warlord nodded. "Come. Leave your guards outside."

Stane entered the tent and stared. The weapon was grey, human-sized, and hanging from wires near the rear of the yurt. It resembled a high-tech suit of medieval armour. It was dented and burnt, nearly destroyed before being pieced back together.

"Stark's escape bore unexpected fruit," the warlord said.

Stane nodded slowly. "So this is how he did it."

"This is only a crude first effort," the warlord said. "Stark has perfected his design." He looked at a set of grainy surveillance photos showing a man in red and gold armour wreaking havoc in Gulmira. "He has made a masterpiece of death. A man with a dozen of these could rule the whole of Asia. You dream of Stark's throne. We have a common enemy."

Stane ran his fingers over the armour, putting his hand through the hole in the chest plate.

"If we are still in business," the warlord said, "I will give you these designs as a gift." He gestured to a battered laptop and reams of yellowed paper filled with drawings and schematics. "In turn, I hope you will repay me with the gift of iron soldiers."

Stane smiled and put his hands on The warlord's shoulders.

For a moment, The warlord looked puzzled. Then he froze in his chair, a victim of Stane's hidden sonic taser.

"This is the only gift you will receive," said Stane.

He removed the earplugs that had protected him from the device's effects. "Technology has always been your Achilles' heel in this part of the world. Don't worry. It will only last for fifteen minutes. That's the least of your problems."

Stane turned and exited the tent. As expected, his men had easily rounded up the rebel troops. The warlord's men knelt, bound and gagged, near the SUVs.

"Crate up the armour and the rest of it," Stane told his lead guard. "We're taking it with us."

Back inside his SUV, Stane made a phone call. "Set up Sector 16, underneath the Arc Reactor," he ordered. "Recruit our top engineers. I want a prototype right away."

CHAPTER 16

Deeming himself sufficiently healed, Tony had gone straight back to work in his lab, fixing his suit.

He called Pepper to go on an errand. "I need you to go to my office," he said, taking a finger-sized gadget from his worktable and handing it to Pepper. "Hack into the mainframe and retrieve all the recent shipping manifests."

"And what do you plan to do with this information if I bring it back here?" asked Pepper, crossly.

Tony shook his head. "Same drill. They've been dealing under the table, and I'm going to stop them. I'm going to find my weapons and destroy them."

"Tony," Pepper said, her voice shaking. "You know that I would help you with anything, but I cannot help you if you're going to start all of this again."

"There is nothing except this," Tony said. "There's no art opening, no benefit, nothing to sign. There's the next mission and nothing else."

"Is that so? Well then, I quit," Pepper said, putting the gadget back on the table.

Tony arched an eyebrow at her. "Really? You stood by my side when all I did was reap the benefits of destruction, and now that I'm trying to protect the people I put in harm's way, you're going to walk out on me?"

"You're going to kill yourself," she said. "I'm not going to be a part of it."

"I shouldn't be alive, unless it's for a reason," Tony said. "I'm not crazy, Pepper, I just finally know what I have to do. And I know in my heart that it's right."

Slowly, Pepper nodded and picked up the gadget again.

She paused and looked at him. "You're all I have too, you know."

Tony smiled.

Pepper hurried through the darkened halls of Stark International. She knew the corridors like the back of her hand. But sneaking around for Tony made her nervous.

Fortunately, she hadn't run into anyone on her way to Tony's office. She turned on his computer and plugged in the device he'd given her.

The gadget quickly began hacking into all the computers in the network. The device located Obadiah Stane's machine and began downloading information from his hard drive. Pepper's eyes went wide as orders for Jericho missiles, shipping manifests, schematics and blueprints flashed on the screen. One file revealed diagrams of a suit that looked just like the one Tony had built. The file was named, 'Sector 16'.

"Sector 16? What are you up to, Obadiah?" she asked quietly.

An icon for a video file appeared onscreen. She clicked it open and watched as the image sprang to life.

The picture showed Tony, very beaten up, tied to a chair in a cave. Thuggish-looking guards surrounded him. One of the guards spoke.

"You did not tell us that the target you paid us to kill is the great Tony Stark. As you can see, Obadiah Stane, your deception and lies will cost you dearly," the brutish man said. "The price to kill Tony Stark has just gone up."

Pepper's jaw dropped and she began copying the files to the small device.

Just then, the office door opened, and Stane walked in. Pepper froze. Did he have any idea what she was up to?

"So, what are we going to do about this?" he said, circling slowly around the desk.

As he did, Pepper quickly switched the computer screen to a harmless screensaver and covered the device with a newspaper. She could hardly breathe.

Stane stood behind her. "I know what you're going through, Pepper," he said. "I was so happy when Tony came home, it was like we got him back from the dead."

He moved to sit on the edge of the desk, next to her. "And now I realize, well, Tony never really did come home, did he? He left a part of himself in that cave. It breaks my heart."

"Well, he's a complicated person," Pepper replied, nervously. "He's been through a lot — I think he'll be all right." She really wanted to get out of there.

Stane looked at her. "You're a very rare woman. Tony doesn't know how lucky he is."

"Thank you," said Pepper, awkwardly. "I'd better get back there."

As Stane turned away for a moment, she snatched the hacking device from the computer and walked quickly out of the office.

"Take care," he said, watching her leave.

Stane clicked the computer mouse, bringing the screen back to life. He narrowed his eyes. Pepper had downloaded his secret files.

As Pepper rushed towards the main entrance, she looked over her shoulder to see Stane watching her from the floor above. Just when she thought he might run after her, she ran into Agent Coulson at the security desk.

"Ms Potts," Coulson said, "did you forget our appointment?"

"No," Pepper replied, latching onto his arm. "Of course not. We're going to have it right now. Come on, walk with me." She picked up her pace and raced towards the door.

As she led Coulson out of the building, Stane hurried off in the opposite direction.

In a sub-basement of Stark International, a group of the company's best engineers were working on Iron Man's old, grey armour, which lay disassembled into its component pieces.

Obadiah Stane threw open the doors and stormed in.

The head engineer looked nervous. "Sir, we've explored what you've asked us and it seems as though there's a little hiccup," he stuttered. "To power the suit — the technology doesn't exist."

Stane put his arm around the engineer, almost crushing him, and pointed at the Arc Reactor.

"Here is the technology," he said, with exasperation. "I've simply asked you to make it smaller."

"Honestly, it's impossible," replied the engineer, quivering.

Stane exploded. "Tony Stark was able to build this in a cave!" He towered over the engineer, prodding his chest. "With a box of scraps!"

"Well, I'm sorry," the engineer said, cowering. "I'm not Tony Stark."

Tony wandered into his living room. His mobile phone was ringing somewhere. He located it under a cushion on the sofa and saw Pepper was trying to reach him.

"Tony, Tony!" she cried. "Are you there?"

Tony was about to respond, when suddenly, paralyzing pain shot through his entire body.

Stane was standing behind him, a sonic taser in his hand. He stepped back as Tony slumped into a chair.

"Easy now," Stane said with a wicked smile. "Try to breathe."

He showed Tony the taser. "You remember this one, right? It's a shame the government didn't approve it. There's so many uses for short-term paralysis."

Stane walked around the sofa and stood in front of Tony. He held Tony's face in his hands.

"Ah, Tony. When I ordered the hit on you, I worried that I was killing the golden goose," Stane mused.

Tony couldn't speak, but his eyes widened in shock.

"But, you see, it was just fate that you survived it," continued Obadiah, opening his briefcase and removing a clamp. He opened Tony's shirt and began removing the RT heart from the socket in Tony's chest.

"You had one last golden egg to give," he marvelled, looking at the Arc Reactor as he pulled it out. He held it up and it cast an eerie glow across Tony's face, which was growing paler by the second.

"Did you really think that just because you have an idea, it belongs to you?" he said, leaning in close. "Your father, he helped give us the atomic bomb. Now what kind of a world would it be today, if he was as selfish as you?"

With that, he tugged sharply at the RT, pulling it violently from Tony's chest, leaving wires dangling from the socket. Tony shuddered.

"Oh, it's beautiful," said Obadiah, sitting down next to Tony and examining the glowing heart. "Your ninth symphony. Your legacy. A whole generation of weapons with this at its heart. They'll help us steer the world back in the right direction – put the balance of power back in the right hands – our hands."

He placed the RT in his briefcase.

"I wish you could see my prototype," he said as he stood up. "It's not as conservative as yours."

As Stane walked away, he had one last thought. He spoke over his shoulder. "Too bad you had to involve Pepper in this. I would have preferred that she'd lived."

Tony sat immobile, gasping for breath.

CHAPTER 17

"What do you mean he paid to have Tony killed?" Rhodey blared. "Why would Obadiah . . . ? Where is Tony now?"

Pepper tried to keep her voice calm as she strode across the car park at Stark headquarters. "I don't know," she said into the receiver. "He's not answering his phone. Will you go to the mansion and make sure he's OK?"

She signed off, glad that Agent Coulson had brought five other agents with him. They'd need a small army to go against Stane and the resources of Stark International.

Her first priority, now that she'd convinced Coulson to help her, was finding out what Stane was up to. 'Sector 16', the high-tech lab below the Arc Reactor, would be the place to start looking. A chill ran down Pepper's spine as they headed for the lab.

Tony gasped for breath as the elevator doors slid open, revealing his workshop. He tried to take a step, but his knees buckled and he fell on his face.

Slowly, painfully, he began crawling across the workshop floor. He could see his goal — encased in Lucite — sitting on the table on the far side of the lab: his old chest piece. Thank heavens Pepper had saved it.

It was less than 50 feet away, but it seemed like miles. Tony's heart pounded in his chest. At any moment, the shrapnel might kill him.

He reached the bench and hoisted himself up, fumbling for the plastic container. He grasped it in his hand. The heart's pale glow illuminated his face. The Lucite was much harder than ordinary plastic; Tony wasn't sure he had the strength to break it.

He raised the container as high as he could and smashed it down onto the floor. The Lucite shattered and the glowing chest piece skidded free. Desperately, Tony wrapped his fingers around it.

Obadiah Stane stepped into Sector 16, the sub-basement lab below the Arc Reactor. In his hand he held the glowing RT heart he'd stolen. The overhead lights were off; everyone had gone home.

The prototype armour – the armour that would make Stark's shareholders even richer – stood in a corner, next to the original armour.

Carefully, Stane opened the new armour's chest plate and locked the stolen heart into place. The sensors in the faceplate of the helmet glowed to life – twin eyes, burning in the darkness. Stane smiled.

Rhodey reeled back and kicked the front door of Tony's mansion off its hinges. Inside, the home was eerily dark and silent; Jarvis didn't greet Rhodey as he entered.

The living room was in a shambles. Furniture lay overturned, several lamps had been broken.

"Tony?" Rhodey called. "Tony?"

There was no answer.

"Tony, where are you?"

Rhodey went to the elevator leading to the lab, but it was locked on the lower floor. He found the stairway and jumped down the steps three at a time.

He saw Tony slumped face-down on the floor next to his worktable.

"Tony!" he shouted, racing over to him. He turned his friend over. Tony looked stupefied, but he was alive.

"Where's Pepper?" Tony gasped, gripping Rhodey's arms for support as he pulled him up.

"She's fine. She's with five agents. They're about to arrest Obadiah."

"That's not going to be enough," said Tony, grimly.

One of Coulson's agents placed explosives on the hinges of the locked door leading to the sub-basement lab. Pepper's pass code wasn't working for some reason, and none of them wanted to waste time trying to figure out why.

The agent finished inserting the detonators into the explosive and called, "Clear!"

Everyone retreated around the corner of the stairwell and crouched down. The agent pressed the control button and the explosive blew the door off its hinges.

Rhodey marvelled as he looked around Tony's workshop. The entire place seemed to have been turned into an armoury. Electronic components lay everywhere. Rows of helmets, boots, and gauntlets filled the laboratory shelves. Two suits of gleaming armour hung in the middle of the room, suspended by cables that were attached to the ceiling.

Tony was getting into his armour. Robotic arms moved around him in an intricate dance, tightening bolts and making adjustments.

"That is the coolest thing I've ever seen," Rhodey said.

"Let's do it," Tony replied. He finished donning the armour and lowered the helmet over his head.

Rhodey nodded. "You need me to do anything else?"

Tony nodded back and said, "Keep the skies clear." With a sound like a rocket lifting off, his boots fired and he soared out through a ragged hole in the workshop roof.

Rhodey watched for a moment, in awe. Then he saw the other suit of armour – the silver Mark II.

"Next time," Rhodey said to himself, with a grin. He raced to the garage on the far side of the lab, picked out the fastest car he could find, and zoomed off, chasing his friend.

Coulson led Pepper and the group of agents through the smoking doorway and into the corridor beyond.

The huge laboratory ahead was dark, lit only by the blinking lights of the automated machinery, which filled the room almost to overflowing. It had been a long time since Pepper had been down here, and everything looked different – sinister.

Coulson shone a flashlight into the gloom and picked out a battered suit of armour – the one Tony had used to escape his kidnappers.

"Looks like you were right," Coulson said. "He was building a suit."

"I thought it would be bigger," Pepper replied, confused. This suit didn't look very sophisticated.

Some chains jangled behind her and she turned to see what looked like empty hooks, high above her.

She suddenly found herself alone, as the agents had separated around the room to investigate. As she peered further into the

82

darkness, she suddenly saw two glowing white eyes staring back at her.

Pepper gasped as the eyes rose to their full height. Facing her was a huge metal suit of armour – much bigger than the one she'd seen hanging in the lab or the one Tony used. It looked like a cross between a man and a tank.

She turned and ran, dodging through the lab equipment, as the metal monster crashed after her. The agents opened fire and bullets burst pipes around her, spewing steam into the semi-darkness. As Pepper raced for the lab door, the armoured giant was behind her, crashing past worktops and throwing agents out of the way.

As Pepper made it through the lab entryway, it shattered into a spray of dust and debris behind her, but she didn't dare look back. She ran up the stairway, slowing to catch her breath only when she reached the third landing.

The wall below her shook as something smashed through the door. But the thing was too big for the stairwell and it got stuck.

Pepper turned and ran as fast as she could.

Meanwhile, Tony was speeding towards Stark headquarters.

"How do you think the Mark I chest piece is going to hold up?" he asked Jarvis.

"The suit is at 48 per cent power and falling, sir. That chest piece was never designed for sustained flight," Jarvis advised.

"Keep me posted," Tony said.

He dialled Pepper, who had made it outside the front doors of the building.

"Tony!" she yelled. "Listen to me – Obadiah, he's gone insane, he built a suit and he, he –"

"I know," Tony replied, "get out of there right now."

Suddenly, the ground beneath her shook. An armoured fist blasted through the pavement at her feet. Another fist punched through, widening the hole. Some hands peeled the asphalt back like a flimsy sweet wrapper.

The armoured form of the Iron Monger burst up through the crater. Pepper backed away, stumbling over the broken pavement. The iron giant towered over her.

"Look . . ." Pepper said, backing away.

The Iron Monger stepped forward, the ground shaking beneath his boots. "Your services are no longer required," he said, as a row of miniature machine guns rose out of his gauntlet, aimed directly at her.

The voice sounded computerized and distorted, but Pepper would recognize it anywhere. She was right. The Iron Monger was Obadiah Stane.

CHAPTER 18

"**P**epper," Tony called, "duck!"
Pepper threw herself flat on the ground, as Iron Man zoomed over her head, activating the repulsors in both hands. The blasts hit the Iron Monger and he staggered backwards. Iron Man kept coming, slamming his fists into the giant's armoured chest.

They smashed through a cement wall and then through the retaining wall that separated the Stark International buildings from the nearby highway. Drivers slammed on their brakes and cars careened out of control as the metal titans crashed down in the middle of the road.

The Iron Monger grabbed a station wagon and hefted it over his head. The family inside the car screamed.

"Put them down," Tony told him.

"Collateral damage, Tony," the Iron Monger replied.

Tony hit his repulsors, but nothing happened; probably they'd been damaged in the fight.

"Divert power to chest RT," Tony instructed Jarvis.

Energy surged through the RT in Iron Man's chest plate. A powerful repulsor burst blasted forth and struck the Iron Monger full in the chest, making him stagger. As the giant fell, he heaved the car towards Tony.

Iron Man caught the vehicle, but the weight forced him to his knees. The armour's servos whirred, but their power had been drained by the massive repulsor blast. Tony's old RT heart didn't have the energy of

85

the new one Stane had stolen.

"Power reduced to 19 per cent," Jarvis said.

Iron Man's armour buckled and the station wagon fell on top of him. The Iron Monger recovered and thundered towards his victim once more.

"Go, Mom! Go!" a kid in the station wagon cried. The woman inside stomped on the accelerator and the car took off, dragging Iron Man with it. Sparks flew as Tony's armour scraped across the pavement.

The Iron Monger followed, stepping on some cars, batting others out of the way. Drivers that were caught on the roadway stopped and fled from their vehicles.

Tony finally managed to pull himself out from under the station wagon. He staggered to his feet, his armour smoking. The Iron Monger grabbed the front wheel of an abandoned motorcycle and smashed the bike into Iron Man.

Iron Man sailed through the air for 100 yards and smashed into the retaining wall right next to a bus. The Iron Monger blasted off, his immense bulk hurtling forward like a cannonball.

The Iron Monger picked up Iron Man, threw him to the ground and pressed one huge boot into his chest.

Tony grunted with the impact and tried to lift the boot off. But saving the station wagon had depleted even more of his power reserves.

With a creaking, metallic sound, the Iron Monger shook his head. "I built this company from nothing," the giant said. "And nothing is going to stand in my way — least of all you."

Iron Monger picked up Iron Man, threw him into the side of the bus and launched a rocket at it from beneath his shoulder plate. The bus exploded in a fireball, shooting Tony into the air — but as he fell back down, he activated his jet-powered boots and stopped just above the burning vehicle.

"Impressive," said Iron Monger. "You've upgraded your armour. I've made some upgrades of my own."

The giant powered up his own boots and rose slowly into the air.

Inside his helmet, Tony grimaced.

"Sir, it appears his suit can fly," Jarvis said.

"Duly noted," Tony replied. He thought quickly. "Take me to maximum altitude."

"With only 15 per cent power the odds of actually reaching that altitude —" Jarvis began.

"I know the math!" Tony interrupted. "Do it!"

He turned and sped upwards ino the night sky, followed closely by Iron Monger.

CHAPTER 19

"**E**leven per cent power," warned Jarvis, as Iron Man climbed higher and higher.

"Keep going!" insisted Tony, determined.

Iron Monger was gaining on him.

Suddenly, Iron Monger grabbed hold of Iron Man's boot and he yanked him close in a choke-hold. The two armoured men faced each other.

"That was a great idea, Tony, but my suit is more advanced in every way," laughed Stane.

"How'd you solve the icing problem?" asked Tony, innocently.

"Icing problem?" said Stane, confused. Iron Monger hadn't noticed that his suit had become frozen and encrusted as he'd reached high altitude. It started to malfunction. The lights in his eyes flickered as he lost power and plummeted back towards the ground.

Tony watched as Stane fell. But he had problems of his own – his suit was now running on back-up power. His boots started to stutter as he made his own unsteady descent back to Stark International, finally crash-landing on the rooftop.

"Potts," called Tony over his comm-link. "I'm almost out of power. I gotta get out of this thing. I'll be right there."

Tony pulled off one gauntlet and was just about to remove his helmet, when the roof behind him shuddered. Tony wheeled around as Iron Monger landed 20 feet away. Flames still licked around his blackened armour.

Tony barely managed to get his faceplate down before the Iron Monger struck.

"Nice try," said Stane, as his huge fist smashed into Iron Man's chest.

Iron Man skidded back across the rooftop and tumbled to his feet. He reached for the controls with his remaining gauntlet, but the Iron Monger caught him in a massive bear hug. Tony gasped as his armour began to crack under the pressure.

"Jarvis," Tony gasped. "Deploy counter measures!"

Instantly, compartments on the armour flipped open and a thousand particles of chaff exploded, filling the air with smoke, flame, and metal.

Surprised, the Iron Monger lost his grip and Tony rocketed free. He landed behind a wall, hidden — for now.

"Potts," Tony whispered into his comm-link.

"Tony!" gasped Pepper, terrified.

"This isn't working," he said. "We're going to have to overload the reactor and blast the roof."

"Well, how are you going to do that?" she asked.

"You're going to do it," he replied.

Pepper looked worried.

"Go to the central console, open up all the circuits," Tony instructed, calmly. "When I get clear of the roof, I'll let you know and you hit the master bypass button. It's going to fry everything up here."

Pepper took a deep breath and headed nervously back through the doors of the building.

"Make sure you wait until I clear the roof," warned Tony, again.

Pepper quickly made it to the console and turned on every single switch she could find.

Iron Man stepped out from his hiding place and leapt onto Iron Monger's back. He reached into the gap between the giant's helmet and body armour and tugged at the machine's targeting system.

"This looks important," said Iron Man, as he ripped the wires out.

The Iron Monger staggered and reached behind him. His metal fingers latched onto Iron Man's helmet. He whirled, tossing Iron Man like a doll.

Iron Man bounced to a halt and Tony gasped as the evening breeze ruffled his hair. The Iron Monger had ripped off his helmet!

The head and body of the Iron Monger opened up to reveal Obadiah Stane seated inside. He laughed as he crushed Tony's de-powered helmet like a tin can.

Iron man staggered to his feet. He and the Iron Monger faced each other. The Iron Monger lumbered forward, and Tony realized, for the first time, that the giant's armour had built-in machine guns.

Tony jumped aside as the Iron Monger sprayed the roof with bullets. The huge glass skylights shattered beneath Iron Man, but without his helmet controls, he couldn't fire his jets.

He caught onto the side of the roof at the last instant. He heard a gasp below him and, glancing down, saw Pepper standing near the reactor core. As Tony clung on, the Iron Monger kept shooting.

Iron Man's armour stopped a few glancing blows, but Tony knew that without his helmet, sooner or later his luck would run out.

"Pepper!" he shouted down through the skylights. "Hit the button!"

"You said not to!" she shouted back.

"Just do it!" Tony cried as another bullet dented his armour.

"But you're not off the roof!"

"Pepper, we have no choice! We have to stop him! Do it now!"

CHAPTER 20

Pepper hit the button and dived for cover under the nearby consoles. A pulse of electromagnetic energy flashed upwards, blasting Iron Man out of its path. Iron Monger, who was standing at the edge of the skylights, was not so lucky. The energy pulse rocketed past him, slamming into the suit and sending electrifying shocks through Stane's armour.

The lab went dark, then the building, then the rest of the Stark International compound. And, on the roof of the Arc Reactor, the power to both suits of armour died as well.

Stane's head hung limp inside the Iron Monger armour. There was a pause, then he sagged forward, tumbling over the edge of the skylight and falling down into the Reactor core.

The impact of the Iron Monger smashing into the core created a final, massive burst of energy, which shot back up to the roof and exploded in a giant fireball. The Iron Monger had vanished forever.

Iron Man lay unconscious where he'd fallen, his RT heart glowing faintly. He'd had a very close call, but Iron Man would live to fight another day.

Days later, Tony was sitting in his office, reading a newspaper which ran the headline, 'Who Is Iron Man?' Pepper stood next to him, dabbing powder on his face to conceal his cuts and bruises, ready for a huge press conference.

"Iron Man . . ." Tony mused. "Not a technically accurate name, since the armour is a gold-titanium alloy . . . But I like the ring of it. 'Iron Man'."

Agent Coulson handed him some note cards.

"Here's your alibi," he said. "You were on your yacht during the whole incident. I've got port papers that put you in Avalon all night and sworn statements from fifty of your guests."

"Maybe it was just Pepper and me," Tony suggested. "Alone, on the island."

Pepper ripped a plaster off his forehead.

"That's what happened," said Coulson, pointing at the statement. "Just read it word for word."

"There's nothing about Stane here," Tony said, flicking through the notes.

"That's being handled," Coulson replied. "He's on vacation. Small aircraft have such a poor safety record."

"But what about the whole cover story that it's — he's — my bodyguard? That's kind of flimsy, don't you think?"

"This isn't my first rodeo, Mr Stark," said Coulson. "Just stick to the official statement and soon, this will all be behind you."

He glanced up at a flat-screen TV, which showed Rhodey delivering his own prepared statement to the press. "You've got 90 seconds," he said, then headed for the door.

"Oh, Agent Coulson!" said Pepper, running after him. "I just wanted to say thank you for all of your help."

"That's what we do," he answered. "You'll be hearing from us."

"From the Strategic —" Pepper began.

"Just call us 'S.H.I.E.L.D.'" He smiled and left.

Pepper turned and hurried Tony to the door, helping him into his suit jacket.

"You know it's not that bad — even I don't think I'm Iron Man," he said, reading through the prompt cards.

"You're not Iron Man, remember?" Pepper said, encouraging him to stick to the statement.

"Fine, suit yourself. But if I *were* Iron Man, I'd have this girlfriend who knew my true identity."

Pepper turned him around to face her, so she could straighten his tie.

"She'd be a wreck," continued Tony, looking intently at Pepper's face. "She'd always be worrying that I was going to die, yet so proud of the man I'd become — she'd be wildly conflicted. Which would only make her more crazy about me."

Pepper was ignoring him, folding a pocket handkerchief, her eyes lowered.

He stopped her suddenly. She looked at him questioningly.

"Tell me you never think about that night?"

"What night?" she sighed.

"You know," nodded Tony, gazing into her eyes.

Pepper smiled slightly. Her tone softened, as she looked back at him, dreamily. "Are you talking about the night that we danced . . . and went up on the roof . . . and then you went downstairs to get me a drink and you . . ."

Tony smiled back at her.

"Left me there, by myself?" she finished, her face hardening again. "Is that the night you're talking about?"

"Hmmm," said Tony, straightening up, embarrassed.

"I thought so," smiled Pepper, tucking the handkerchief into his pocket. "Will that be all, Mr Stark?"

"Yes, yes," he said gruffly, "that will be all, Miss Potts."

Tony walked through the side door and onto the stage that had been assembled in the lobby. Rhodey was finishing his speech as Tony arrived.

"I can confirm that a series of military test prototypes were involved in the incident at Stark International last night," Rhodey said. "And now, Mr Stark has prepared a statement. He will not be taking any questions."

Tony walked to the podium and motioned for silence. The sea of reporters quietened down. He duly started to read the statement that had been prepared for him.

"There's been speculation that I was involved in the events that occurred on the freeway and the rooftop –"

"I'm sorry, Mr Stark," interrupted Christine Everhart, who was sat in the front row, glaring at him. "Do you honestly expect us to believe that was a bodyguard in a suit, that conveniently appeared?"

Tony frowned. "I know it's confusing," he said. "But it is one thing to question the official story and another thing entirely to make wild accusations or insinuate that I'm a superhero!"

"I never said you were a superhero," countered Ms Everhart.

"Didn't you?" faltered Tony. "Well, good," he continued, awkwardly, "because that would be outlandish and, well, fantastic." He let out a sigh and tried to recover from his mistake.

"I'm just not the hero type. Clearly. The mistakes I've made, largely public . . ."

"Just stick to the statement," Rhodey whispered in his ear.

Tony nodded and looked at his prompt cards again.

"The truth is . . ."

He paused. He looked out at the expectant press and made a decision.

". . . I am Iron Man."

As the crowd erupted into a cacophony of questions, Tony Stark smiled. For Iron Man, this was only the beginning.

The Stories of the Iron Man and Iron Man 2 Movies

2-in-1 Novel

IRON MAN 2

+

IRON MAN

Published by Sunbird Books Ltd 2010
A Penguin Company

Penguin Books Ltd, 80 Strand,
London, WC2R 0RL, UK
Penguin Books Australia Ltd,
Camberwell, Victoria, Australia
Penguin Group (NZ), 67 Apollo Drive, Rosedale, North Shore 0632, New Zealand
(a division of Pearson New Zealand Ltd)

ISBN: 978-1-40939-014-5
10 9 8 7 6 5 4 3 2 1
Printed in Great Britain

IRON MAN 2

Written by Alexander Irvine
Based on the Screenplay for 'Iron Man 2' by Justin Theroux
Based on the Marvel Comic

CHAPTER 1

A massive aircraft soared through the sky. Below it, lights flashed and people screamed. When Iron Man tipped himself out of the cargo door of the plane and began soaring towards the ground, an observer might have thought he was diving into a war zone. But no...this was more like a Hollywood movie premiere.

It was opening night of the Stark Expo, a show sponsored by Stark Industries that brought together the best and brightest minds from around the world to share ideas and new technologies.

The crowd on the Expo grounds poured into the Tent of Tomorrow. They had already been treated to a montage, on the giant video screens, of Iron Man's recent exploits: an aerial tango with a barrage of shoulder-fired missiles, a lightning raid on a pirate ship off the Horn of Africa, a head-on collision with an air-to-air missile, whose explosion coming over the Expo sound-system was loud enough to register on nearby seismometers. The crowd loved it.

And they exploded at the sight of Iron Man falling from the sky to execute a perfect somersault at the last moment and land at the centre of the stage.

Robot arms sprouted from the stage and formed a framework

around Tony Stark, unlocking the invisible joints on the Mark IV suit and lifting it away from his body. From the crowd's perspective, it appeared that Iron Man had been disassembled and a tuxedo-clad Tony Stark constructed in his place. The whole procedure took only a few seconds. Tony was a genius inventor and billionaire who had created the Iron Man suit so that he could help people and fight the evils of the world.

"It's good to be back!" he called out over the tumult. He paused for a moment to get his breath. Six months earlier, when he'd turned himself into the armoured superhero, he hadn't known what a physical toll it would take. Between the explosions, the late nights and the recent problems with palladium, Tony Stark was not the man he had once been. But he had a show to put on.

"Ladies and gentlemen," he began. "Decades ago, my father, Howard Stark, began a grand tradition. Every ten years, he would level the playing field for inventors by building a city. An idealized city. A city of the future. An Expo where for five glorious months, scientists, world leaders, and corporate CEOs could come together to pursue one goal: advancing mankind."

The giant TV screen behind him lit up with archival footage of the first Expo. The camera panned across visions of the future ranging from the fanciful — Your Children's Flying Car Is Here Today! was one slogan that drew a laugh from the crowd — to the hardheaded and practical, all against the backdrop of the New York City skyline.

"A place to do the impossible," Tony said. "A place to unleash

ideas." Howard Stark appeared on the screen, shown in his workshop sometime around 1970.

"Everything is achievable through technology," Howard Stark said in the old film footage. "Better living, robust health, and—for the first time in human history—the possibility of world peace!" He gave the camera a nervous smile as he walked to a scale model of that first Expo. "And everything you'll need in the future can be found right here. So from all of us at Stark Industries, I'd like to personally show you the City of the Future…the Stark Expo! Welcome."

Applause from the crowd swelled over Tony's father's speech. Tony himself picked up the thread. "Today I'm issuing a challenge. A challenge for anyone, any country, any company to prove its value. A chance to put up the best ideas, the best inventions…the best foot forward, in the hopes of leaving the world a better place than the one we came into." With a bow and a flourish, he headed for the stage exit. "That's all I've got for now. Have a good time!"

As he spoke the last words, the lights cut to black. The music picked up where it had left off, booming through the darkness as the crowd went nuts all over again. The Stark Expo, bigger and better than ever, was under way.

In a forgotten part of Russia, a flickering television screen showed Tony Stark's grand entrance at the Expo. It was quite a spectacle: flashing lights, loud music.

Ivan Vanko watched. He was alone except for the TV and his cockatoo, Irina. His father, Anton Vanko, had passed away recently. Since then Ivan had turned his small apartment into a workshop, filled with welding equipment, spools of wire and bits of metal.

His father had told him many things – and shown him many things. Ivan had learned the true stories of Anton Vanko's work and Tony Stark's crimes. Ivan had absorbed as much of his father's knowledge as he could. He had sorted through old records and plans, notebooks and loose sheaves of paper covered in diagrams and equations.

Ivan shuffled through boxes of his father's papers and brought out a cardboard tube. On the peeling label he read the English words: Stark Industries. Underneath were two names: Howard Stark and Anton Vanko. It was time for Ivan to claim his heritage and for Tony Stark to learn the bitter truth about his own. Ivan returned to the work table and spread out the blueprints in the spill of lamplight. The words 'Arc Reactor' filled him with a sense of purpose. Tony Stark believed the Arc Reactor was his own invention. Ivan couldn't wait to see the look on Tony's face when he realized how wrong he was – for that alone Ivan Vanko would have given his life. But Tony Stark was arrogant and full of pride, and Ivan didn't think it would ever occur to Tony that someone could be his intellectual equal.

At least, not until it was too late.

CHAPTER 2

Happy Hogan was there to meet Tony as he came offstage. "How'd it go?" Hap asked.

Tony shrugged. "I've done better."

"This way, sir," Happy pointed, and they immediately headed through the wings to the backstage meeting and media area.

Tony signed a replica of an Iron Man mask for a little kid and scribbled a few other autographs. Then Happy hustled Tony down the corridor towards the backstage doors. Tony was running out of petrol — fast.

"Let's get out of here," Tony said as he staggered from exhaustion. Happy grabbed his friend and held him up. Looking around to see if anyone had noticed Tony's stumble, Hap asked, "You OK, man?"

"Aces," Tony said. He'd started to notice odd discolourations around the Arc Reactor housing in his chest. Tendrils of a sickly purple colour radiated out of it. Put that together with the unpredictable bouts of weakness and he was pretty sure he had a big problem.

Tony had his artificial intelligence program, Jarvis, trying to find a new power source for the reactor in his chest. The palladium fuel cells that currently glowed inside it were clearly poisoning him.

Happy shoved open the backstage door and a fresh wave of shouts and flashes greeted them. Tony rose to the occasion, shrugging off Hap and playing to the crowd as they manoeuvred towards the car. Happy triggered the remote control that opened the roof of Tony's favourite set of wheels—a grey sports car. Tony grabbed the key from Happy. "I'm driving," he said.

As he settled into the driver's seat, a ravishing brunette appeared next to the sports car.

"Pleased to meet you, Mr Stark," she said.

Tony had no idea who she was. "You, too, Miss...?"

"Marshal," she said.

"I'm Tony, Ms Marshal, and you are...?"

"US," she said, and slapped an envelope onto his chest. "You are hereby ordered to appear before the Senate Armed Services Committee tomorrow at nine am," she said. She let go of the envelope and turned away.

Tony turned to look at Happy, who was reading over the court summons. "Do I really have to go to that?"

"This?" Happy said. "Yeah, I think you do."

It was not the first time Tony had testified before the Senate, but he had a feeling it was going to be the least pleasant. He was at a table by himself. His primary antagonist was a certain Senator Stern, who was currently speaking to him.

"I'm sorry we're not seeing eye-to-eye here, Mr Stark, but

according to these contracts, you agreed to provide the US taxpayers with," – Stern flipped through a file and read – "'all current and as yet undiscovered weapons systems.' Now, do you or do you not at present possess a very specialized weapon –"

"I do not," Tony said firmly.

"You are not in possession of said weapon?"

"It depends on how you define the word 'weapon'," Tony said.

"The Iron Man weapon," Stern said.

"My device does not fit that description."

"And how would you describe your device?" Stern's tone of practised weariness grated on Tony.

"A high-tech prosthesis."

Stern became angry. "The Iron Man suit is the most powerful weapon on tl e face of the Earth," he said. "Yet you use it to sell tickets to your theme park."

"My father conceived of the Stark Expo to transcend the need for war by addressing its sole cause: the coveting of resources," Tony said. "Primarily energy. If your priority in this hearing was truly the safety –"

"Our priority is for you to turn the Iron Man suit over to the military."

"I am Iron Man," Tony said. "The suit and I are one."

The senator decided to try a new tactic. "I'd like to call upon Justin Hammer, our current primary defence contractor, as an expert witness."

Justin Hammer strode down the aisle. His tie was a bit loose, his trousers a bit tight, his hair flopping over his forehead as he nodded at acquaintances on his way to be sworn in. He ran Hammer Industries, a huge rival company to Stark Industries. Since Tony had stopped making weapons, Hammer and his company had stepped in to supply the US Government. But the rivalry hadn't ended.

Tony turned his focus back to the committee. "Let the minutes reflect," he said into the microphone, "that I observe Mr Hammer entering the chamber and am wondering if and when an expert will also be in attendance."

Senator Stern's gavel banged over an outburst of laughter. If Hammer was bothered, though, he didn't show it. "I may well not be an expert. But you know who was?" he asked, playing to the gallery but addressing the question to Tony. "Your dad, Howard Stark — a father to us all, and to the military-industrial age. And just to be clear: he knew that technology was the sword, not the shield, that protects this great nation. A sword that when rattled can calm threats from foreign lands and slay dangers before they arrive on our shores."

Hammer went on. "Anthony Stark has created a sword with untold possibilities, and yet he insists it's a shield! He asks us to trust him as we cower behind it! I love peace, but we live in a world of grave threats. Threats that Mr Stark will not always be able to foresee."

Tony rolled his eyes. Anthony? Nobody had called him Anthony since maybe the first day of nursery, which he'd gone to only because

other kids did.

"We can't let a similar technology be created by a country far less moral than our own," Hammer said. "Believe me, ladies and gentlemen, when I say that Mr Stark keeps the secrets of that suit at the peril of our citizens."

Tony had an idea. He slipped his new Personal Digital Assistant out of his pocket. It was a rectangle of fibre optics, pure computing power that looked like a piece of clear plastic. He started fiddling with it while Senator Stern continued. "Thank you, Mr Hammer. The committee would now like to invite Lieutenant Colonel James T Rhodes into the chamber."

Tony looked up, towards the door, where Rhodey was entering in full dress uniform. He looked uncomfortable.

Tony met his best friend in the aisle and shook hands with him. Tony was glad to see Rhodey there. If there was any living human Tony knew he could count on to do the right thing, that person was James Rhodes.

After Rhodey had been sworn in, Stern said, "I have before me a report on the Iron Man compiled by Lieutenant Colonel Rhodes. Colonel, please read into the minutes page fifty-four, paragraph four."

"Certainly, Senator," Rhodey said. "May I first point out that I was not briefed on this hearing nor prepared to testify—"

"Duly noted," Stern said without looking up from his notes. "Please continue."

Rhodey swallowed the snub and went on. "This paragraph out of

context does not reflect the summary of my findings."

"Did you or did you not write 'Iron Man presents a potential threat to the security of both the nation and her interests'?"

By way of answering, Rhodey continued and completed the quote. "'As he does not operate within any definable branch of government.' However, I went on to recommend that the benefits far outweigh the liabilities —"

"Thank you, Colonel Rhodes," Stern said.

Undeterred, Rhodey finished his sentence. "And that it would be in our best interest to fold Mr Stark into the existing chain of command."

"Colonel Rhodes," Stern went on, "please read page fifty-six of your report."

Rhodey glanced at the indicated page and gestured to a bank of monitors, which lit up to display blurry satellite images. "Intelligence suggests that the devices seen in these photos are in fact all attempts at making manned copies of Mr Stark's suit." With a laser pointer, he indicated points on each of the monitors where blurry images showed something like an armoured suit.

Enough, Tony thought. He fired up the mini virtual desktop on his PDA and set to work getting some visual evidence that would actually prove something — even if it wasn't what Stern and his colleagues had set out to prove.

"This has been corroborated by our allies and local intelligence on the ground," Rhodey went on, "indicating that they are quite possibly,

at this moment, functional."

Tony stood and touched an icon on his PDA. "Let's see what's really going on here," he said as his PDA took control of the monitor screens. "If…I…may," he began, as a series of classified videos — some of them existing only on intranets behind security walls that the Department of Defence would never get through — loaded and began to play. At top left, a North Korean testing site was hosting a test flight of a skeletal suit. Something like Tony's repulsors fired, lifting suit and pilot into the air. "Wow, it looks like I have commandeered your screens," remarked Tony with a smile.

"And you're right," he continued. "North Korea is well on its…" Suddenly, the suit and pilot disappeared in a flash of light that overwhelmed the camera. When the image resolved, the smoking remains of the suit were being hosed down by firefighters. "Nope," Tony said. "Phew. That was a relief."

Similar results played out on the other monitors. "Let's see how Russia is doing … Oh, dear," Tony went on. "And Japan?… Oh, I guess not. India? Not so much. Germans are good engineers. Yowch. That's gonna leave a mark." Then he froze all the looping videos except one. He expanded that image until it took up the entire bank of monitors.

"Wait," Tony said. "The United States is in the game, too. Look, it's Justin Hammer." Glancing over his shoulder at the camera crews filming the hearing, Tony added, "Hey, guys, you might want to push in on Hammer for this."

What unfolded on the single remaining video was a comic disaster. Hammer stood off to one side of the frame as a crew strapped someone into an armoured exoskeleton. Obviously, it had been constructed with the Iron Man suit in mind, but Tony could tell by looking at it that the weight distributions were all wrong for the location of the propulsion systems. On the monitor, Hammer stood back and winked at the camera.

The real-life Justin Hammer in the Senate chamber looked as if he had a mouthful of spoiled milk. On the monitor bank, Hammer's prototype suit lifted off into the air over the proving ground and started a loop-the-loop that quickly turned into a spiral. The thrusters cut out with the operator moving parallel to the ground, and pieces of the prototype started to fall off. He landed in a sitting position, kicking up a huge plume of sand. Hammer could be heard yelling to cut the video.

In the Senate chamber, Hammer stood. "I would like to point out," he said, "that the test pilot survived and suffered only minor spinal bruising. He is currently white-water rafting with his family."

Senator Stern pointed his gavel at Tony. "By making a mockery of this hearing, you are short-changing the American people!" he bellowed.

Tony turned to face the camera. "The good news is," Tony said, "I'm your deterrent. The goal of the suit is not to use it. And it's working. You're welcome. I have successfully privatized world peace. Not that I'm above throwing on the suit and breaking up an international bar fight

here and there. You want my property. You can't have it. I try to play ball with you. Something goes wrong overseas, I get the three am call. My bond is with the American people, whom I will always keep safe."

And there was the gavel, hammering down as Stern said "Adjourned!" and rose to stalk off the committee dais. Tony hopped down from the lectern he'd taken over, flashed peace signs, and blew kisses. The cameras loved him.

Fool, thought Ivan Vanko. He was working while watching Tony Stark's Senate hearing on TV. And he was carrying on an occasional conversation with Irina, the cockatoo.

He was nearly finished.

Ivan's eyes watered and his neck ached from hunching over the fine soldering work required in the construction of a functioning miniature Arc Reactor. Until that exact moment, only two had existed in the world. Now there was a third, tiny and perfect, glowing on his worktable as if it possessed secret knowledge. This was a moment his father would have loved. Ivan wanted to share it with someone, so he reached out one hand towards Irina's perch and waited for her to climb onto his knuckles.

"Isn't it beautiful, Irina?"

The bird chirped.

Ivan Vanko had made an Arc Reactor. He was the second man in history to do so. It would forever gall him that Stark was the first, that Stark had suppressed Anton Vanko's pioneering work and then

16

taken sole credit for further developments. Ivan would have to console himself with being there when Tony Stark was destroyed.

The Arc Reactor fit perfectly in the palm of Ivan's hand. He plugged it into the ancient desktop computer he had scrounged out of the trash and ran a diagnostic program he had written. All of the Arc Reactor's processes were happening exactly as they were supposed to, within the parameters he had sought.

The Arc Reactor glowed. Irina cackled. Outside, the sun was setting and snow was beginning to fall. Ivan began to piece together the next part of his plan.

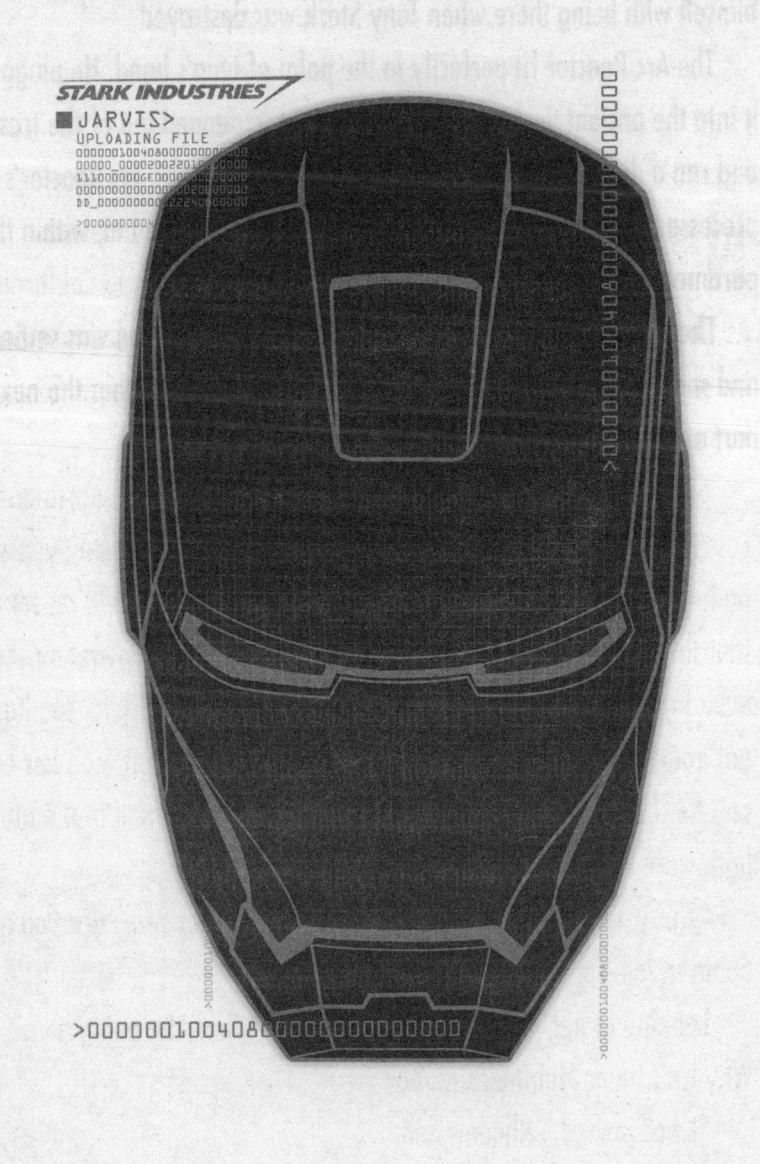

STARK INDUSTRIES

■ JARVIS>
UPLOADING FILE
000000100408000000000000
00000_000020502010000000
111000000GE00000000000000
000000000000000000000000
DD_00000000022240000000
>000000000

CHAPTER 3

No good deed goes unpunished. Pepper Potts's good deed was inviting Rhodey to catch a ride on Tony's plane back to California. As Tony Stark's assistant, Pepper helped with all things relating to Stark Industries and to Iron Man. Her current assignment was to get Tony home from the Senate hearing.

Since Rhodey was stationed at Edwards Air Force Base, north-east of Los Angeles, and since he and Tony had been friends for many years, and since their friendship was currently strained, Pepper had reasoned that there were several good reasons for extending the invitation. And even knowing Tony's occasional propensity to act like a child, she had not anticipated the current situation. She sat in a seat between her boss and her boss's best friend. Neither one of them would talk to the other; both were feeling betrayed. Both wanted an apology.

"This is ridiculous," she finally said. "Are you for real? Are you not going to talk for the entire flight?"

Looking at her, Tony pointed at Rhodey. "What's he doing here? Why isn't he on Hammer's plane?"

"I was invited," Rhodey said.

"Of course he was invited," Pepper said, assuredly. "Rhodey is

always welcome."

"Not by the owner of the plane," Tony said. "And that's bad jetiquette. Guests are not allowed to invite other guests."

Rhodey tried again. "Tony—"

"I'm not a guest," Pepper interrupted. A warning tone crept into her voice.

"Can you tell him I'm not talking to him?" Tony said.

"Then listen," Rhodey said. "What's wrong with you? Do you know that showing classified footage on national TV is—?"

"No worse than stabbing your best friend in the back at a Senate hearing?" Tony broke in. "How about a heads-up next time?" He pointedly gave Rhodey the cold shoulder by turning to Pepper.

But Rhodey wasn't finished. "I gave you the report! I asked you to fact-check it!" he protested.

"Did not," said Tony.

"He did," asserted Pepper.

Tony glared at both of them. "Like I would even remember," he said with a wave of his hand. "You still owe me an apology."

"I wouldn't count on it," retorted Rhodey.

Pepper interrupted before the argument could get any worse. "Tony, let's go over your schedule. Can we schedule the call with the secretary-general of the United Nations? It's embarrassing that we missed—"

"Let's talk about my birthday party," Tony said.

Pepper took a deep breath. She wondered how long it would take her to hit the ground if she jumped out of the plane at that exact moment. "I recommend that in keeping with the times, we do something small, elegant," she began.

"I don't follow trends—I set them," Tony said. "We're gonna have a huge party."

Pepper forged ahead. "Monaco," she said. "I think we should cancel." The Monaco Historic Grand Prix car race was one of Tony's favourite biennial rituals.

"Absolutely not," Tony said, exactly as Pepper had anticipated. "I've entered a car in the race." Which Pepper knew, of course. She had seen the financials on the car. Stark Industries had spent a mint on maintaining Tony's vintage race car.

"Great," Rhodey said, with enormous false enthusiasm. "I won't be there. We can 'not' have lunch together."

"What? You're not going?" Tony looked suspicious.

"I don't think we should hang out right now," Rhodey admitted. "It's bad for our friendship."

Tony looked away, out of one of the windows.

There was silence as the jet began its descent. Rhodey wanted what was best for the United States, and to him the Iron Man suit was the culmination of a long tradition of US military superiority driven by technological innovation. Tony was privately of the opinion that much of Rhodey's hard-line attitude about Tony's actions came from simple

jealousy. Rhodey wanted a suit. It was that simple.

"Next time," Tony said, "you're flying commercial."

Once he got home, Tony went straight into his lab to work with Jarvis on testing new combinations of possible power sources for his chest repulsor transmitter. Jarvis was trying all sorts of chemical combinations in an effort to improve the formula. But the tests kept failing. The palladium was proving to be toxic to Tony's body.

"Rise in palladium levels," Jarvis said. "Biological toxicity now at 22 per cent."

Bad news. Tony sighed as he traced the purple lines spreading from the centre of his chest. They were thicker and longer. Some of them had sprouted smaller lines that wandered off to meet each other, creating a webbed effect.

He heard someone on the stairs and looked over his shoulder to see Pepper tapping her code into the access panel at the lab door. Tony quickly buttoned up his shirt and picked up one of his new inventions, a Tech-Ball, tossing it around nonchalantly as he turned to meet her.

"What were you thinking?" Pepper snapped without preamble as soon as she was through the door. Her words took Tony aback just a bit, but of course he couldn't let her know that. "Just now?" he said. "If a doughnut was the size of a washing machine, would I be able to take a bite out of it?"

Pepper ignored his reply. "Did you just donate our entire modern art collection?"

Tony had, in fact, made the donation. At least he had ordered it done, and he thought that his orders had been carried out. But because he was in a literal mood, he decided not to commit to an answer about which he could not be 100 per cent certain. "I'm not sure," Tony said. "I didn't physically check the crates."

"We curated that collection for more than ten years!" Pepper said. He could tell that she was purely baffled. So was he, actually. Why had he done that? "It's worth more than six hundred and eight million dollars!" added Pepper.

Tony shrugged. This was not a persuasive line of argument. "Of my money."

"It's tax-deductible," Pepper said. "Why didn't you check with me?"

"Can I do it? See, I'm checking with you." Tony let the Tech-Ball bounce off the desktop.

"Check with me before you do it," Pepper said.

"Is it OK, then?"

Pepper gave up. "Yes, it's OK."

Tony nodded. "Good. Think fast."

As he spoke, he tossed the Tech-Ball to her. Reflexively, she reached up to catch it—but instead of slapping into the palm of her hand, the Tech-Ball turned inside out, wrapping around her hand like a cocoon.

"I don't want to play ball with you," Pepper said after a moment. The Tech-Ball turned back into a ball. Setting it down, she said, "There are a hundred other things to talk about. Which category would you

like to start with? Stark Industries?"

"Not yet," Tony said.

"Iron Man," Pepper said.

Tony shook his head. "Love it, but pass." What was there to talk about? Iron Man was Iron Man.

"Expo?" Pepper asked.

Ah. That's more like it, Tony thought. He nodded. "Shoot."

"Wind farm initiative, plastic tree plantation, solar retrofitting..."

"Whoa!" Tony held up a hand. He couldn't deal with all of this right now. But he was pretty sure he knew someone who could. And she was standing right in front of him. He paused, wondering if the time was right. He decided it was.

"I'm giving you a promotion," Tony announced. "Do you accept?"

Pepper froze. Her face ran through six different expressions. "Are you serious?" she asked. Tony just blinked at her. "You...you are serious," she said. "I—yes! Yes, I accept!"

"Congratulations, Ms Potts," Tony said, shaking her hand. He meant it.

"I have so much to do," she said. Turning on her heel, Pepper hurried from the room. Tony turned back to his palladium problem.

CHAPTER 4

After hours of more failed tests, Tony decided to vent some of his frustration by taking a boxing lesson from Happy. He'd had a boxing ring put into his home gym just for this purpose.

"Cover," Happy said, after sticking a jab into Tony's nose. "Don't drop. Hands up. Jab-jab-hook-uppercut-jab."

Eyes watering from the jab, Tony threw the combination.

Happy flicked the punches aside and said, "You're dropping your hook. Again."

Tony heard the doorbell ring and a moment later looked up to see Pepper walking into the gym. "The messenger is here with the paperwork for my promotion," she said.

"Great," Tony said.

A young woman he had never seen followed Pepper into the room.

"Natalie Rushman, Mr Stark," Pepper said. "Mr Stark, Natalie Rushman."

"Pleased to meet you, Mr Stark," Natalie said. "And congratulations, Ms Potts."

Tony invited Natalie up into the boxing ring. She climbed up and tried to hand him some papers to sign. "How long have you been with Stark, Natalie?" Tony asked.

"Ah, barely six months," she answered. "In legal." Tony looked her up and down. Then he hopped out of the ring and went over to one of the many holographic computer screens he had around the house. Tony pulled up Natalie's résumé from the Stark Industries' personnel files. What he saw impressed him.

Natalie held out a pen and the stack of forms, trying again. "You need to sign, Mr Stark."

Going back to the ring, Tony nodded. He signed the papers quickly and handed them back.

"Well! It's official!" Pepper said. "Off you go, Miss Rushman, and thank you for bringing those by."

Pepper walked Natalie out and then headed back into the gym. Tony made no effort to keep the admiration out of his voice. "Did you see her résumé? Fluent in French, Italian, Russian...Latin? Who speaks Latin?"

"I know where this is going," Pepper said, "and no. I'll be hiring my own replacement."

"Hire her."

Ivan could have chosen any of a thousand different ways to destroy Stark, but in the end Ivan's chosen weapon was the whip. His creation was five feet long, made of articulated tungsten carbide vertebrae. He had machined each vertebra himself and linked them together onto a woven cable. A handle, insulated and wired to the power supply,

extended another 6 inches.

Deactivated, the whip lay on his worktable. Ivan wound copper wire around the vertebrae, weaving it along the cable and through holes like the nerve openings in a spinal column. When the weapon was done, Ivan Vanko would possess a whip of white-hot molten metal. Not even Stark's armour would survive it for long. Nothing could. Ivan finished wiring the whip. He shrugged into a harness he had built of leather-wrapped tungsten and placed the miniature Arc Reactor in a housing set over his sternum, mimicking the Iron Man chest plate.

He ran the cable from the glowing chest repulsor transmitter down his arm to the handle of the whip, attaching it at the shoulder, the bicep, and the radius. Before he plugged in the RT, Ivan put on a glove; even with the insulation, he did not expect to be able to hold the whip bare-handed. The glove extended well up his forearm and would protect him from accidental grazes of the whip.

Taking the whip in hand, Ivan stepped away from the table to a clear space in the middle of the floor. He plugged the power cable into the whip. It sparked to life with a hum that shook Ivan's bones and a crackle that he could feel pressing on his eardrums. He flicked out the whip, and bits of plasma jumped from the tip, searing holes where they landed. Irina squawked and fluttered her wings, scooting to the end of her perch farthest from the light and noise.

Glancing around the room, he caught sight of the television replaying highlights of Tony Stark's Senate hearing. Ivan flicked

the whip away from his body and then pivoted to bring it down in a sweeping arc. The sight and sound of it connecting with the TV was like a lightning strike with thunder. His ears rang, and his eyes watered from the flash. An involuntary grin spread across his face as he blinked away the tears and looked at what he had done.

The TV now lay in two roughly equal halves — the ancient screen and tube had exploded into sprays of glittering fragments. Ivan had not felt a thing, no sense of resistance or even impact. His grin broadened. He flipped the whip in a tight loop as if spinning a lasso. The tip sparked, leaving a gouge in the floor. He touched a stud on the inside of his wrist and the whip shut off.

Now that it was operational, Ivan decided to build a second whip.

CHAPTER 5

A few days later, Tony took all of them to Monaco for the big car race. While Happy parked the limousine, Tony, Pepper, and Natalie went into a fancy hotel restaurant to watch the race. Tony had overruled Pepper and had hired Natalie as his assistant, and he was pleased with his decision so far. Natalie's fluent French saved them when they tried to order drinks from the waiter.

As Pepper looked around the room, she saw TVs mounted everywhere, airing pre-race coverage. Then she spied Justin Hammer walking across the room. Tony spotted him, too, and sniffed in disgust.

"Tony!" Hammer boomed on his way to the table. Hammer inclined his head at Pepper and said, "I just wanted to pop over and congratulate Ms Potts on her promotion."

"Thank you," Pepper said.

Hammer turned to Tony. "I'm actually hoping to have something to present at your Expo this year," he said.

"Love it!" Tony said. "Just so you know, we're mostly highlighting inventions that work."

"Don't count me out," Hammer said. "Maybe you haven't heard, but you're not the only rich guy with a fancy car in the race this year."

"Really? Look alive, then. I have a pretty decent driver this time around."

On the TV screens, the crowd noise ratcheted up. Cars were moving into position. "Looks like we're about to see who's got the better man," Tony said. "Now if you'll excuse me, I'd like to freshen up before the ball."

Tony zipped out of the room before anyone could stop him. It was race day! Tony was ready to enjoy it.

Hammer had wandered to another table with some business associates. He glanced up at the TV to see whether the race had started. What he saw on the screen made him gasp.

On the screen, in high definition, big as life, was Tony Stark, getting into a car with the Stark Industries logo on it. He was suited up like the other drivers. He settled into the car and placed the steering wheel just the way he wanted it.

Hammer's mouth dropped open, then clamped shut. He couldn't believe that Tony had upstaged him again!

On the TV, Tony winked and shot a thumbs-up at the worldwide audience, then roared off towards the starting line. The English-speaking announcers noted that the world was going to find out whether Tony Stark could drive a race car as skilfully as he designed and built them.

Although he couldn't understand a word of French, Hammer could hear tone of voice in any language, and he could tell that the French

30

announcers were going crazy. He heard another gasp across the room and noticed that Pepper had just seen the television screen, too. She must not have known about it.

That Tony Stark, thought Hammer, *really knows how to keep a secret.*

CHAPTER 6

How Ivan loved machines. All machines. In Ivan's veins ran the blood of a born engineer. His father, too, had been destined for engineering greatness. A Stark had derailed that plan. Ivan would get it back on track.

Engines roared to life around him. He faded into the crowds of technicians and journalists who stood back, their jobs done for the moment, and watched the drivers run last-minute checks. One after another, the cars headed to the starting line.

As the race began, Ivan got ready, putting on his harness and two whips. When the time was right, he threw off the overcoat he'd been wearing and strode directly towards the track.

Ivan's left-hand whip slashed through the chain-link fence under the grandstand as if it weren't there, leaving a gouge in the sidewalk. Two more flicks of the whip, right and left, opened a section of fencing so that Ivan could walk through it. He came to the safety barrier bordering the track, a three-tiered metal railing that offered little more resistance than the chain link had. He slashed a V-shaped opening through it as one of the cars thundered by, the wind of its passage rocking Ivan and blowing his hair across his face.

In the hotel restaurant, viewers saw that the TV cameras were

focused on the disruption on the racecourse. Someone had invaded the track and was using a kind of electrified rope to hack away at the passing cars. He was big, with long, lank hair and a kind of metallic exoskeleton frame that linked his two—ropes? cables? whips?—to a power source that glowed at the centre of his torso.

"The Monaco Historic Grand Prix is making history for quite another reason," said the lead announcer. "Who is this guy? He must be stopped!"

Cars were crashing into each other and piling up around the invader as they tried to avoid him. "That can't be good," Pepper said. She was trying to figure out how he was doing whatever he was doing. Then she saw that the guy on the track wore what looked suspiciously like a miniaturized Arc Reactor.

Happy walked in. "What's going on?" he asked.

"Where's the football?" she said quickly. He held it up—an aluminium briefcase lacquered in the same deep red as the Iron Man suit. They had given it the code name 'football'. It was shackled to his arm.

Pepper stood. It was time to make sure Tony wasn't in over his head, for the millionth time. She told Natalie to arrange a plane to get Tony out of the country fast, and then turned to Happy. "Let's go."

Hurrying to the limo, Pepper said, "Give it to me." Happy handed her the key and held out his arm so she could reach the lock on the football. She worked at it as they ran together out of the hotel and

toward the VIP lot.

The briefcase held a lightweight 'travel' version of the Iron Man suit. They'd never done a field test of it, but Pepper thought this might be the time. Now if only she could get the key to work. "Hold still, Happy," she said.

"What, and run at the same time? You try it," Happy said, but he held his arm steadier as they ran. When they got to the limo, Pepper still hadn't opened the lock. With one arm, Happy drove in the direction of the track while Pepper jerked the football around, this way and that, trying to unlock the handcuff that was attached to his other arm.

"Drive faster!" she said. "And hold still so I can get this key to work."

Left behind in the restaurant, Natalie spoke into her mobile phone. "He's going into turn ten."

She looked around to confirm that Hammer was riveted by the escalating mayhem on the track, and that Pepper and Happy had left the room.

While she talked on her phone, Natalie tried to track what was happening on the racecourse with Tony. "He is extremely vulnerable at the moment," she said.

She was extremely vulnerable at the moment, too. Her support network was a long way off, and it would be very easy for a misunderstanding of her operational role to escalate, compromising her

mission. That could not be allowed to happen.

Natalie held the phone, listening for another moment, and then said, "Understood," and hung up. After allowing herself to relax for a moment, she dialed her phone again. The one thing she could do at the moment was make sure that the Stark Industries plane was ready to go when Tony was.

Oblivious to the disruption on the track, Tony was racing around the course, having the time of his life. He had just passed Hammer's car and knew that the driver would be looking at his rear bumper for the rest of the race. He smiled.

Suddenly, he saw the cars in front of him veer crazily away from something in the centre of the track. Just before one of the cars disappeared in a fireball, Tony could have sworn he saw a man... and something sparking, like live wires.

The fireball cleared, and Tony saw that there was a man on the track, walking against the direction of the race. He was big and muscular. From his hands dangled a pair of whips that glowed and sparked as he flicked them against the concrete.

The car in front of Tony braked and swerved. Tony stayed behind it, using it as a shield. A flickering line of energy shot out and destroyed the car, splitting it just behind the seat. The two parts of the car, spitting vapours and flame, tumbled into the crash barrier. Now Tony really pushed on the brakes, but there was no way he could avoid the guy on

the track. He hauled on the steering wheel, felt the car shudder into a skid, and watched in what felt like slow motion as the man flicked one of the whips towards Tony's car.

The whip sheared through the chassis and split the car into two pieces, which slid along the track. Tony came to a stop, upside down in the front end of his car. He popped the steering wheel loose and flipped it out onto the track so that he could wriggle out of the driver's seat. His helmet had cracked in the crash and he stripped it off. The remains of his car rested between him and the man with the whips and the metal exoskeleton.

At that moment, Ivan reached the wreckage of Tony's car and slashed it methodically into small pieces, the whole time shouting in a language that sounded to Tony like Russian. Tony waited for just the right moment, then grabbed hold of the nearest bit of wreckage and swung it at the back of Ivan's head.

Tony put everything he had into the swing. It was a good one. The blow landed solidly . . . but had no visible effect.

Tony paused, switching tactics to psychological diversion. "Are we beyond talking this through? Finding some common ground?"

The whip man roared like an animal and slashed at the space recently occupied by Tony Stark. But Tony was already off and running, looking for cover. All he saw were pieces of race cars, beautiful machines turned into expensive junk.

One car lay upside down at an angle that would provide brief cover.

Tony ran from the whip man quickly enough to stay alive but slowly enough to keep the pursuer coming. Then Tony dove under the car. He yanked off the petrol cap and scrambled forward, away from the stream and splash of high-test fuel.

There was petrol everywhere, and a crazy man approaching with whips that apparently made fire. Tony got away just as the whip guy was close enough to strike.

The whip slashed down through the car's engine and into the track surface, coming into contact with the spreading pool of fuel. The explosion that followed blew the car to unrecognizable pieces and sent Tony pinwheeling into a wall of hay bales at the edge of the track. He started to right himself and looked back towards the dissipating fireball.

There was the whip man, walking through the flames as if they weren't there and coming towards Tony as though he were the only thing in the world that mattered.

"I see Tony!" Happy cried out. He had charged through the gate and had driven onto the track. He and Pepper were moving against the direction of traffic—but there was no traffic anymore. There were hulks of destroyed cars, pit crews running onto the track to save drivers, spectators rushing up and down the stands in waves. There was fire on the track, everywhere.

Happy lost sight of Tony. A fireball on the track hid everything. Happy floored the limo and headed that way.

"I think I have it!" Pepper yelled, still twisting at the lock on

his wrist.

There was Tony again.

Happy took in the situation all at once. Tony was down, half-buried in a collapsed pile of hay bales on the inside of the crash barriers. He was moving, though. A big area of the track near Tony was on fire. Through the fire came the big nutcase with the laser whips, cracking them on the pavement and grinning at the sound.

There was one thing to do, and Happy did it. He cut the wheel hard and hammered down on the brake, sending the limo into a fishtail spin and smashing the bad guy with the back end. The limo slammed hard into the crash barrier, crumpling the railings and setting off the air bags. The vehicle came to a rocking halt, still running. It had pinned the guy to the wall.

What to do next? Happy wondered. He was about to open the door, when he noticed the boss approaching the limo.

"You got the football?" Tony asked before Happy had a chance to lower the window all the way down—but it didn't really matter, since the spider-webbed glass disintegrated as soon as he hit the button.

Pepper finally popped open the lock and raised the briefcase to show him.

"Thanks," Tony said.

"You're welcome," Pepper managed.

As Tony reached for the case, the car lurched. The maniac reared up from behind it and, with a barbaric yell, whistled one of his whips past

Tony's head. The whip tore through the armoured hood of the car as if it were aluminium foil. Tony spun away. The whip man slashed at the car to free himself. He hacked away at the boot and the rear tyres, his whips even slicing into the backseat.

From the limo, Pepper called out, "Tony!" She opened the door and slid the football across the slick pavement in his direction. Then she and Happy ran from the track.

Incredibly, the lunatic whip man, who was wearing—could it be?—an RT on his chest, had hacked away enough of the back end of the car that he was almost loose. He kept at it until, with a final heave, he shoved free of the limo's bumper and stalked through the wreckage after Tony.

By the time he reached the billionaire, however, the situation had changed dramatically. Tony caught the football and entered a code into a pad next to its handle. It chirped its acceptance. He opened the case and placed one foot in either half. Then the football proceeded to build a light, portable version of the Iron Man suit, the Mark V, from the boots up around Tony's body. It wasn't the same as the full apparatus, but it was still a formidable piece of body armour.

The first crack from an energized whip left deep scoring in the suit. Tony dodged the next several swings and goggled at the RT on the whip man's chest. How is that possible? Tony thought. The glowing RT and the Arc Reactor technology were so Stark-proprietary that even the Department of Defence had never touched the tech. Who was this guy

who had just shown up in Monaco and started wrecking the place with his RT-powered whips?

A whip sparked across Tony's torso, coming dangerously close to his own RT. Tony grabbed the arm holding the whip and flung the man into the smoking wreckage of two cars. He pounded the whip man every time an opening arose. He barraged him with pieces of cars, pieces of track — anything close at hand. Tony got in close and delivered punches until he could feel the heat from the whips. He danced away, then started the attack again.

His heart was pounding. He was tired. *Time to end this*, Tony thought as he threw himself into a clinch with the villain, pinning him down and just plain pounding him until the man quit. Breathing heavily, Tony tore the RT from the whip wielder's chest and looked at it. He couldn't quite believe what he saw.

Suddenly, police swarmed on the lunatic destroyer of the Monaco Historic Grand Prix, who smiled as the officers dragged him away. "I win," he said to Tony.

Tony walked off the track, looking at the RT, fascinated by it. It shouldn't have been possible, but there it was.

"Pepper," he said, "we need to get to the plane and test this."

"Test it? This is the most important thing we can do right now?" Pepper replied.

"As a matter of fact, it is," Tony said. "See, that's because this thing cannot exist. Because if it exists, that means someone out there

has access to either my servers or my brain. Neither of those things should be possible. Perhaps we can find out what really has happened, once our Russian pal is interrogated. But if he doesn't tell the police anything," Tony said, holding up the RT, "this will. So, yes, we need to test it. OK?"

"OK," Pepper said.

CHAPTER 7

By the time Tony Stark walked into the local police station, he'd run some preliminary tests on the RT recovered from 'Whiplash' — as the media had already named him — and the results were startlingly similar to Tony's own design.

In the hallway, Tony stopped a French prison official who was on the phone. "...Russian, but he speaks English," he was saying. "No. All we got was a name."

When the official hung up the phone, Tony asked, "Who is he?"

"Not sure yet. We're assuming he's Russian."

Tony tried to think of any Russians who might want to put together energized metal-filament whips to hurt him — and who might be able to build an RT. None came to mind. "I need to talk to him," Tony said.

The official let Tony into the holding cell where a manacled Ivan — Tony had caught the prisoner's first name on his way in — sat with his back to the door. Ivan was a big man, even without the RT apparatus and the whips.

"Is that you, my friend?" Ivan said softly. Tony didn't answer. Ivan shifted his weight but didn't turn his head. "Tony Stark?"

Tony walked around to where Ivan could see him. He held up the

RT. "It's pretty good," Tony said, and meant it. "Where did you get it?"

As Tony spoke, Ivan's eyes drifted shut, and he tipped his head back. A smile spread across his face. "You like it?" he said. There was no mistaking the pride in his voice. "I'll make you one."

"You didn't make this."

Ivan's smile got a bit wider. "It wasn't so hard."

Tony took a step towards Ivan. "Who made this?"

Opening his eyes, Ivan looked Tony in the eye and laughed. "Your technology is built from stolen goods. You come from a family of thieves."

'A family of thieves.' Tony committed that to memory. What did this Ivan know about his family, or think he knew? "Where did you get it?" he asked again.

"It came from the past. From Anton Vanko," Ivan said reverently.

"Who's that?"

Suddenly enraged, Ivan surged against his manacles. "It is a name you should know!" he shouted.

"Why?"

Ivan cooled off. The ethereal smile returned, now with a bit of a predatory edge. "It's killing you, isn't it?"

He knows, Tony thought. How could he know? This was a problem Tony had never thought he would encounter: someone else independently arriving at tech he'd thought was his own. Well, his father's; the initial designs for the Arc Reactor came from old blueprints

Tony had found in his father's lab after the old man died.

He looked back at Ivan and saw that Ivan was studying him.

"It's. Killing. You." Ivan touched his forehead, at the temple. "I know these things."

For one of the few times in his life, Tony Stark was speechless.

The French official entered and held the door. "Time's up," he said.

Ivan leaned his head back and closed his eyes again. He seemed happy. "Goodbye, Tony Stark," he said.

Three hours later, a guard arrived at Vanko's cell door and tapped on it to let Ivan know to stay back while he opened it.

The guard looked up and down the hall to make sure it was empty. For a moment Ivan thought there would be a fight, and that was fine with him. Then the guard set down a tray next to Ivan, caught the prisoner's eye, and nodded. Ah, Ivan thought. An unexpected twist to events.

"Eat up," the guard said in Russian. Then he left, locking the cell again.

Ivan took a look at the food. Mashed potatoes—but it didn't smell like mashed potatoes. The next thing Ivan noticed was something he initially thought was a digital clock with a malfunctioning display. It said '30'. Then it said '29', then '28'... and Ivan put it all together. He knew what the mashed potatoes were, and he knew what this small LCD device was, and he understood why the guard had left it all here, and he knew that if he didn't act now, he was going to die.

The detonator read '24'.

Ivan slapped the mashed potatoes up against the wall and stuck the detonator in the centre of the gooey mass. It said :17. He turned back to the door just as the guard opened it. Ivan followed the guard down a hallway.

Just as they ducked into a stairwell, the charge went off back in his cell. A thunderous boom echoed through the prison, creating a perfect distraction. Sprinklers kicked in, soaking Ivan to the skin as he headed down the stairs at the guard's direction.

Who was this benefactor? Ivan could not think of a single person on Earth who could reasonably be expected to take a risk on his behalf.

Three floors down, Ivan came to a fire escape door. And he was free.

CHAPTER 8

Back at Stark Industries, Rhodey had arrived to talk to his friend. Pepper and Natalie were busy fielding calls from the press, and they waved him down to the lab.

Rhodey got to the bottom of the stairs and peered through the glass walls. Tony stood at his virtual desktop, with a blizzard of holo-projected files walling him off from the rest of the lab. He wasn't looking at Iron Man schematics or breakdowns of engines, though. He was pulling gigabytes of old video footage, photographs, scanned-in reports... Rhodey couldn't quite see how they fit together, and he wouldn't find out until he asked, so he knocked.

Tony glanced up and let him in.

"You OK?" Rhodey asked.

"Yeah," Tony said. "Jarvis, start tapping the grid in New York."

"You look awful," Rhodey said, partly to provoke Tony and partly because it was true. Tony ignored him.

"We need to talk," Rhodey said. "That guy has changed the game. Someone else has your technology. You need to share the suit with us."

"There's no problem!" Tony said, too loudly. "The guy was a one-off. Jarvis, what's the hold-up?"

"That guy was beating you in real time," Rhodey said. "You said it's

46

twenty years before someone else would figure out your technology, but that guy had it yesterday. You need to make a statement."

Tony nodded and started moving. Rhodey followed him up the stairs and into the kitchen, where they could hear the ongoing media disaster from the living room. "You're going to have to issue a press release," Rhodey said. "Soon."

"Sure thing," Tony answered.

Tony walked outside and hailed a news helicopter that was circling his house. "Hey!" he shouted. "Iron Man won! That guy was toast. The world is safe! Iron Man is back on watch!"

Rhodey rolled his eyes. "Really?"

"I think it was effective," Tony shot back.

Rhodey looked at him with annoyance.

As they walked back into the house, Tony finally got serious and put his hand on his friend's arm. "No one understands better than I do the value of what I own. Caving in at this moment and giving over my tech would be a betrayal of what it represents. The government doesn't need my suit. What it needs are more guys like me, not more suits like mine." Tony let go of Rhodey's arm but maintained eye contact. "I created the suit to keep the peace. You need to trust that I take that very seriously."

He waited for Rhodey to say something. When Rhodey didn't, Tony added, "We good?"

"Yeah," Rhodey said, and he meant it, mostly. "I think I just needed

to hear you say that."

"Cool. I'll see you at my party," Tony said.

Tony was true to his word. His birthday party was a huge event. While the celebrities and other guests started to arrive downstairs, Tony was still up in his room. He had asked Jarvis to run another test on his RT. "How we doing, Jarvis?" Tony asked. "Am I really healthy, or just really, really healthy?"

Jarvis gave it to him straight. "Biotoxicity is at its apex. Further strains placed on your body will result in almost certain d—"

"Thanks." Tony cut him off and stood there absorbing the news. Maybe he should have programmed a kinder personality into Jarvis. It was harsh to hear words like that. Depressing. He felt angry and stood there stewing until he heard Natalie calling from one of the walk-in wardrobes.

"I can't find it," she said.

Tony rallied. "No problem," he called back. "Bring anything."

"There are sooo many," she said, carrying an outrageously bright-coloured tie. She looped it around his neck and started tying it. "Voilà," she said, buttoning his collar and tightening the tie perfectly. "I'll go downstairs and make sure everything is ready," she said, flipping open her phone as she left.

"Thanks," Tony said. "You're a gem."

Natalie had seen the discoloration spreading across the upper

48

part of Tony's chest and the base of his neck and had put two and two together. Was the RT doing something to him? If so, he was going to need some serious technical assistance, and there weren't too many people who could provide it. She made a phone call and started talking. There were people who needed to know about the situation — and who needed to be ready to take action.

A while later, Pepper walked into the party, taking in the huge crowd and the fast beat. She sighed and made her way through the packed house, looking for Tony. She found him in the kitchen showing Natalie how one of his Iron Man gloves worked.

"Happy birthday," she said. "I was just stopping by."

Having freed the gauntlet from Natalie's hand, Tony was now putting it on his own. "Nonsense," he said. "We're going to dance."

Which was the last thing in the world Pepper wanted right then, but as usual Tony got his way. The music had segued into something slow, and they walked onto the dance floor.

Before the song ended, Rhodey appeared, carrying a wrapped gift.

"Happy birthday," Rhodey said, handing it to Tony.

Tony flipped the gift up into the air and blew it apart with a repulsor blast from the glove he was still wearing, showering nearby guests with glass fragments. Rhodey stared at him in shock.

"I don't need gifts," said Tony.

Tony walked off, gesturing to spin up the tunes again. Something techno and bouncy got the partygoers hopping, but Pepper and Rhodey

didn't join in. They stood, motionless, in the middle of the dance floor. Around them, the party surged anew. Pepper looked in the direction in which Tony had gone.

"I can't...I just don't know what to do, Rhodey," Pepper said. "Tony is not himself. He's using his suit as if it were a party favour."

"It can't be this way," Rhodey agreed. "It's not safe."

Pepper bit her lip.

"I can handle this," he said. "Go home. I'll take care of it." He watched her walk towards the door, saying brief goodbyes to acquaintances as she went. Then he approached the sound system and turned off the music.

"OK," he said, his voice booming into the sudden silence. "It's twelve-oh-three, so Mr Stark's birthday is officially over. Now it's just another Tuesday. Get out."

People muttered to each other. Most of them started moving in the general direction of the door.

Then Tony, wearing the Mark IV Iron Man armour with the face shield up, reappeared in the partygoers' midst. "Party is over! After party starts now!" he cried, and a cheer went up. Tony seemed determined to act irresponsibly for the evening.

That was it for Rhodey, though. Decision time, he thought. Rhodey turned and left the room. He was about to do something that Tony might never forgive, but for the life of him, Rhodey couldn't figure out what else to do. He remembered Tony saying that what people needed

was not more suits like his but more guys like him. Right now, Rhodey held the opposite opinion. One Tony Stark was plenty. More than enough, in fact.

But one Iron Man suit was not enough at all. Not nearly.

Tony turned to see something he'd never thought he would see. There stood Rhodey, in Tony's own Mark II grey metal suit, in Tony's own house, embarrassing him in front of his guests.

"Time for bed," Rhodey said. He looked serious.

"You know that's mine, right?" Tony said.

Rhodey nodded. "I do."

"Just checking," Tony said.

He slapped Rhodey's arm away and gave him a two-handed shove into the opposite wall. With a thrust-assisted spring, he caught Rhodey before he could get back to his feet; their combined weight and momentum was too much for the wall, and they blew through it into the gym.

They grappled in the boxing ring. Tony uprooted a corner post and swung; Rhodey got one of his own, and the two of them went at it like broadsword-wielding medieval knights until the posts were too bent and broken to be useful anymore. Then Rhodey blew Tony through the wall with a repulsor blast, and the fight moved on to the bedroom. Tony went after Rhodey again and the two of them crashed through a walk-in wardrobe and the wall behind it, bursting into the kitchen in a flurry of punches. Tony finally collapsed in a pile of armour, and

Rhodey was left standing.

Rhodey's head ached from the impact on the suit's helmet, and his body felt like one big bruise. He flew away from the ruins of Tony's house in the suit, knowing that his actions would change the nature of their friendship—maybe even end it. Forever.

He had wanted to believe Tony's spiel about being committed to using the suit for the right reasons and protecting it from those who shouldn't have access to that kind of technology. The world would have been a better place if that were true. But the world wasn't like that, and Tony Stark was not that kind of man. Rhodey could be sad and disappointed about it, but he knew his duty.

Edwards Air Force Base was 90 miles away. Rhodey called ahead, using a direct line to Major Julius Allen. Their conversation was brief. When he landed in a hangar at Edwards 15 minutes later, the major was still yelling at everyone in sight. "I want this entire area on lockdown!" he shouted at a lieutenant. "Get those guys out of here! I want only necessary personnel!"

Rhodey flipped up the suit's face shield and walked towards the major, who saluted him.

"Major," Rhodey answered, with a nod. "Let's talk inside."

Chapter 9

It was morning. Tony didn't like mornings, as a general rule. Warnings from Jarvis about the dangers posed by palladium poisoning, and the certain knowledge that Rhodey had betrayed him to the generals who would turn the Iron Man suit into...whatever they were going to turn it into, were making this particular morning worse. The only thing making it bearable was the box of jam doughnuts in his lap.

Tony wasn't sure how he'd gotten into his dressing gown, or who had delivered the doughnuts, but he knew who had demolished the kitchen – himself. He didn't want to think about it. He munched on a doughnut instead.

"Mr Stark," someone called from the living room. "I'm going to have to ask you to please put down the doughnut."

"I got five more," Tony said, with a mouthful of jam.

"Don't make me come in there," the man said as he entered the kitchen. The stern-looking African-American wore an eye patch and a black leather jacket.

"Oh, brother," Tony said. "Aren't you the guy I kicked out of my house a while back?"

"We were going to have this conversation sometime," said the

bald-headed man. "Now seems like a good time."

Tony shook his head. "Not interested. I have a lot on my mind." He turned his attention back to his doughnuts.

After a brief silence, Eye Patch tried again. "How about I buy you a cup of coffee?" he said pleasantly.

Tony was intrigued. Ten minutes later, fresh coffee was brewing in Tony's fancy coffeemaker. Good thing it had survived the previous evening's fight.

"Who are you again?" he asked Eye Patch.

"I'm Nick Fury."

Tony vaguely recalled the name, but he stopped trying to remember where he'd heard it before when his assistant Natalie Rushman walked in and poured the coffee for him. She was dressed in a dark, navy blue bodysuit. She looked tough as nails.

"Cream and sugar," she said, setting down the cup in front of him.

Tony looked back and forth between Natalie and Fury.

"Pleased to meet you, Mr Stark," Natalie said. "My name is Natasha Romanoff."

Natasha Romanoff? Tony took that in. So Natalie was not what she seemed. "Good assistants are so hard to find," said Tony. Especially assistants who weren't really spies.

"I was asked to keep an eye on you," she said. "To protect you. I'm sorry I lied, but I needed a cover so I could stay close to you without arousing suspicion."

It sounded good, but Tony still wasn't sure he could trust her. Or Nick Fury.

"Tony, I'm the executive director of S.H.I.E.L.D. – the Strategic Homeland Intelligence, Enforcement, and Logistics Division," explained Fury.

Tony nodded. He remembered hearing that before. "Want a tip? Fire your namer of things, because that's a mouthful."

"Our namer of that particular thing is dead," Fury said.

"Problem solved," Tony said. Then he sipped his coffee.

"Your father named the organization," Fury said.

Tony opened his mouth, then shut it again. He didn't want to believe it, because if he did, he had to believe some other things about his father that didn't quite square with the image of Howard Stark that Tony carried around in his head.

Fury was looking at him. "Have I got your attention?" he asked. "Your father was one of the founding members of S.H.I.E.L.D. There are a lot of things you don't know about him. Things about yourself, too."

Tony sat down in a chair. He gathered his bathrobe around him and said, trying not to overreact, "I know all I need to know about myself."

"Oh, really," Fury said. "And what's—"

"I'm dying," Tony said. He pulled back the lapels of his dressing gown to show Fury the discoloration and skin eruptions that now spread from the RT all across his chest and shoulders.

Fury looked closely. "Your body is rejecting it?"

"It is rejecting my body," Tony corrected him. "The tech is strong. I'm the weak link. I'll be dead by the end of the year."

"Time to get better, then, Iron Man."

"Believe it or not, I've already looked into the getting-better thing."

"And?"

"I would prefer it. But it's not an option."

"It's the only option," Fury said. "You're Tony Stark. You built that suit. You said you were Iron Man. Like it or not, you're the future. And unfortunately, the future is a lot bigger than you. Time to cowboy up."

He put something on the table while still looking Tony in the eye. Tony glanced down and saw a roll of sixteen-millimeter film and an envelope. "What's this?"

"You ever wonder why you built your Expo?" Fury asked.

Unable to help himself, Tony opened the envelope. Inside it was a black-and-white photograph of a forty-ish man taken sometime in the 1950s or early '60s, if the surrounding tech was anything to judge by.

"Who's this?" he asked.

"Anton Vanko," Fury said. "He worked with your dad."

Whiplash's father! This was a shock. "I didn't see this in my files," was all Tony could think of to say.

"Because it was in our files." Fury paused so Tony could absorb the information. "Your father was working on things bigger than just weapons for the military," he went on. "Your father saw the future. Which is why he came and worked for us."

57

"What do you mean?" Tony asked.

"Sometimes people are born before the world is ready for them," Fury replied. "Leonardo da Vinci invented the helicopter before anyone had even predicted flight. Howard Stark made a few predictions, too. He was just born way too early to execute them. The world had to play catch-up. And now we're here."

Tony had always believed that his father was a genius. But to hear his father mentioned in the same breath as Leonardo da Vinci... that was strange. Tony wasn't sure how to react, and he also wasn't sure what Fury meant the comparison to convey.

"What do you mean?" he repeated.

But Fury had given him all he was going to give him. He tapped a finger on the film canister and said, "The world has just caught up. Howard's grasp was a lot bigger than his reach." Fury stood. "That's where you come in. And if you don't, someone else will."

CHAPTER 10

Ivan's mysterious benefactor flew him to the United States and was funding his work. This person had an entire fleet of drones—and all Ivan had to do was build RTs for them.

Ivan took it all in. One week earlier, he had been working in two rooms with illegally tapped power and a computer he'd scrounged from someone else's rubbish. Now he was looking at perhaps 3000 square feet of gleaming white space. There were more computers than he could imagine needing to use. At a glance, he saw tools for smelting, machining, welding, wiring, plating, microwave circuit manufacture ... all types of building processes, large and small. *If my father had been given the use of a lab like this,* Ivan thought, *he would have changed the world.*

But Stark had taken away that glory. It was now up to Ivan Vanko to reclaim it.

Much of the lab's floor space was taken up by long rows of gleaming metal drones, humanoid in shape and visibly armed. Ivan walked to the bank of computers that lined one wall of the lab. Before he could make any decisions about the drones, he needed to know how they were put together.

While the data compiled, he examined one of the drones. It had a

humanoid exoskeleton, with a large empty space inside the torso. The drones were his soldiers. They needed some work, but they would do nicely.

One of these, Ivan thought, *will be the last thing Tony Stark ever sees.*

Unless — and this was the only more desirable possibility — the last thing Stark saw was the apparatus Ivan Vanko was building for himself.

A staff sergeant gathered a select group of Air Force engineers who had been waiting in the machine shop attached to the hangar where the Mark II lay on a table. Rhodey, with Major Allen at his left, stood next to it and nodded at the engineers as they came in. These were the Air Force's best and brightest combat engineers, together with a few lab guys who were there to glean what technological goodies they could while they were putting together the new version of the suit.

"What you will be weaponizing," Rhodey told the assembled team, "is a flying prototype of the Iron Man Mark II, for the purposes of an offensive footing."

"Yes, sir," the engineers said, more or less in unison. The engineers approached it, wrenches and screwdrivers in hand. One of them picked up the helmet.

"Don't forget," Rhodey said. "This thing was made by Tony Stark. You're not going to learn everything." He unscrewed the suit's RT and held on to it, just in case. "We're just arming it."

As the engineers got to work, Justin Hammer slammed in through the machine shop door and walked straight to the Mark II.

"You have got to be kidding me!" Hammer exclaimed with excitement. "I got here as quickly as I could."

Rhodey shook hands with Hammer and said, "You think you could hook it up?"

While they were greeting each other, Hammer's men were bringing in an array of crates and setting them near the Mark II.

Hammer winked and popped the lid off the closest crate while his men opened the rest. Before them was a huge array of weapons, including what looked like a miniature cruise missile with onboard continuous command-and-control systems.

Rhodey looked it all over. "Done deal," he said, after a brief – and calculated – pause. "Get busy."

"Which ones do you want?"

"All of 'em," Rhodey said on his way out of the hangar. All of a sudden, he had a lot to do.

Tony Stark was a collector of outdated technologies. Luckily, one item in his collection was an old 16-millimetre film projector. Tony spooled the film Fury had left for him, and started it up.

"Everything is achievable through technology," Howard Stark said, just as he had on the archival Expo footage Tony had shown at the new Expo's opening ceremony a couple of weeks earlier. "Better living,

robust health, and for the first time...sorry...the first..." He burst out laughing. Getting himself back to his mark, he waited while the film crew got ready to do the shot again.

Off camera someone said, "OK, and action, Howard!"

"Everything is achievable through technology," Tony's father began again. He trailed off. After about 5 seconds, the crew started to chuckle.

"I'm sorry, Ron. Let's finish this tomorrow," Howard said.

"Cut," said the off-camera voice. The screen went blank...

...and then came to life again, with a pyjama-clad Howard Stark in his laboratory with an Expo model behind him and a baby cradled against his shoulder. It was dark, and much of the lab was in shadow. "This is the third night you've kept me up with your crying," said Howard Stark to his son. "Thought I'd give your mother a rest. Right now you haven't mastered English yet, so I thought I'd put this on film for you," Howard went on. "I want to show you something."

He stepped aside to let the Expo model fill the frame. "See that? I built that for you. Someday you'll figure it out. And when you do, you'll achieve even bigger things with your life. I just know it. You're the future."

Nick Fury had said the same thing. Only not in the same way. Tony started to shake off his sentimental response and engage his intellect. This footage was his father sending a message, and he expected Tony to figure out what it was.

"I've created so much in my life, but you know the thing I'm proudest of?" Howard was talking to the baby Tony, but now he looked directly into the camera. "You. My son."

Yeah, Dad, Tony thought. *I love you, too. What are you trying to show me?*

And there it was.

There it was! Something at the edge of the frame caught Tony's eye. Scrambling in the semi-darkness for a pen, he jammed it into one of the projector's spindles, stopping the film. Watching carefully, his entire mind focusing on the puzzle his father had sent him, Tony wound the filmstrip back manually, frame by frame, until he saw it again.

Behind his father was the scale model of the first Expo he had used when pitching the project to the relevant authorities in New York City. Something about the shape, the organization of the buildings…it went with what his father was saying. Tony wound the film slowly, slowly enough that he could see each of the still frames and check the tiny differences between them.

There. Tony leaned forward, tracing his finger along the edge of the frame.

At the moment Howard Stark was saying "the future", the shape was clear. The structures looked as though they were arranged the way the atoms might be arranged in a certain molecule.

"He knew," Tony said. "Jarvis, I'll be right back."

Tony ran to the office to grab the Expo model and was back in a

flash. He set it up in the lab. On the virtual desktop, he projected an image of the film frame at the end of his father's out-take—the one with the partial image that had begun to make the shape, and his father's plan, clear to him.

Looking at it, Tony realized the lab setup he had wasn't going to do the trick; the power draw was going to be immense, and he had a hunch he was going to need a lot more computing power than was available in the house network.

Tony went out to the garage and came back draped in cables and carrying a sledgehammer. He dropped the cables in a pile, closed his eyes for a minute to dredge up the memories of how he'd wired the house, and then looked at the wall in front of him.

"Jarvis," he asked, "is this a load-bearing wall?"

"No, sir," Jarvis said.

Tony tightened his grip on the sledgehammer and started swinging.

CHAPTER 11

Forty-eight hours later, the Mark II was transformed.

"I think you will be very impressed," Rhodey said as he walked with General Newcomb into the hangar, where the major and the crew of engineers were assembled. "Major Allen, would you mind doing the honours?"

Allen saluted and walked to the tarp that hung from a frame of two-by-fours. After a glance back at Rhodey, he pulled down the tarp with a flourish. All present caught their breath.

The suit had the burnished silver hue of the original Mark II, but now the outline bristled with weapons. Rhodey ran through the specs: heads-up and communications capabilities derived from highest-grade military packages, combined with the existing protocols Tony had built in during initial development. Arming this suit was the next step in maintaining peace. At least, that's what Rhodey tried to tell himself.

"Unbelievable," General Newcomb breathed. "What do you even call something like that? It's like a . . ."

"It's a war machine," Rhodey said.

At first Newcomb couldn't take his eyes off it. After a while he managed to tear himself away from the War Machine and get down to the business of asking the kind of questions generals were supposed to

65

ask. "Is it functional?"

"One hundred per cent online," Rhodey answered.

"Good." Newcomb faced Rhodey and Major Allen. "The Pentagon has asked that I issue your first orders. Hammer is doing a weapons presentation at the Stark Expo," Newcomb said, cutting Rhodey off with a look. "We'd like to introduce the suit."

The problem, of course, was that when Rhodey had brought the Mark II to Edwards Air Force Base, he had done so with the understanding that the military was creating—in terms both Tony and Justin Hammer had used—a shield rather than a sword. General Newcomb, by making the War Machine a centrepiece of Hammer's presentation at the Expo, was redefining its function. He was turning the War Machine into an aggressive threat instead of the behind-the-scenes trump card Rhodey had intended.

"With all due respect, General," Rhodey said, "I feel strongly that we use the suit only when absolutely necessary."

"Colonel, the world needs to see this," the general said. "Fast. I assure you it is absolutely necessary."

Rhodey said nothing.

"It's also an order," the general finished.

And that was the end of the conversation. "Yes, sir," Rhodey said.

"And very nice work, gentlemen!" General Newcomb beamed at the assembled team. "You've made your country proud."

Tony was using the shape of his father's Expo model as the basis

for an entirely new molecule. He was trying to create something from nothing, so Tony had rigged up a crazy system to ramp up enough power. The parts included a set of mirrors designed to focus anything that hit them on a single, specific point in space; a cube of pure glass whose position in space included the specific focal point of the set of mirrors; a high-energy laser array with beams focused and intensified by the mirrors; and, finally, a centrifuge designed to spin and initiate high-energy reactions. The system was complicated—but that's why Tony Stark was a genius.

He ran checks, and everything was exactly according to spec. The only thing left to do, really, was run the experiment and see whether it would work. Could he create a new type of molecule?

"Jarvis, spin up the non-ferrous centrifuge," he said, and then added, "Be ready to capture whatever floats through it." As Jarvis spun up the centrifuge, Tony ran through his internal checklist again. He'd performed every step. If this was going to work, he'd find out now.

"Let 'er rip," he said.

The laser array flared to life, first in a deep red and then modulating in frequency well up into the ultraviolet range.

"Fingers crossed," Tony said.

The centrifuge hit its target acceleration. Tony was about to tell Jarvis to spike up the energy delivery of the lasers, but Jarvis knew the experiment better than Tony did. Jarvis had already carried out the command before Tony could speak it.

Zap!

Tony was holding his breath. The lasers had gone cold, the centrifuge had spun down to silence, and the glass cube at the centre of it all sat in a sterile enclosure with a tiny grain of imperfection at its centre.

Tony exhaled, long and slow. "That's it, Jarvis," he said. "Scan it."

"Dissecting now."

"As soon as you get its atomic structure," Tony said, "tell me what the name—"

"Unknown element," Jarvis said. "Contains similar transgenic properties to the chemical compound vibernum. Also has characteristics known in uranium. Suggested denomination for the periodic table: Vb 32."

This was good. This was what he had hoped for, even though he wasn't yet sure it would save him. "Name it," Tony commanded.

"Vibranium," Jarvis said, with as much emotion as he ever displayed about anything.

Perfect, Tony thought. "Project it!" he said. A three-dimensional image appeared on the desktop, endless interlocking triangles joined into a perfect sphere.

"It's beautiful," Tony said. "Gimme an RT." An RT diagram appeared. Tony tinkered with it, creating interfaces with the new molecule and seeing how it all fit together. "Spin it," he said. It spun and emitted light. Tony started to think that he might actually have done the impossible. "This might actually work," he said, and set about finding out.

Several hours later, he had managed to cobble together a new triangular Arc Reactor and a sleeve that went inside the existing RT socket. He set the RT against the rim of the socket. It fitted. It looked good.

"Jarvis, what do you think?" he said.

"Eminently triangular, sir," Jarvis said.

It gleamed, with the vibranium power source generating roughly twice the power that the previous palladium compound had provided — and with less than five per cent of palladium's troublesome leaching property.

"Teleconference incoming," Jarvis said.

"Who is it?"

He glanced aside to set the new RT out of the field of the teleconference view and saw the screen open out of the corner of his eye. "What do you want?" he said, not caring who it was on-screen.

Then he saw the face of Ivan Vanko, now known as Whiplash. Tony could see that he was in a workshop or lab. A mess of wires and computers was visible behind him.

"Tony," Ivan said, "today is the day the true history of the Stark name will be written. As thieves. At your own Expo, the world will learn what kind of criminal you really are."

"Let me tell you, Ivan, as one guy with daddy issues to another," Tony said. "I don't think this day is going to turn out the way you want it to. At the end of it, I'm still going to have the Expo and Stark Industries."

"Today, Stark," Ivan said, and then cut the connection.

CHAPTER 12

Natasha was sick of playing Natalie, but Fury had said in no uncertain terms that Pepper Potts was not to know of her undercover infiltration. So here she was, with a headset and a clipboard, waiting around the entrance to the Tent of Tomorrow for Pepper to show up and sit down. Hammer's demonstration was due to start in 15 minutes.

The Tent of Tomorrow was a tent in name only. In reality, it was an open auditorium space under a soaring glass roof, with a high-tech stage and an even higher-tech backstage setup. The backstage area was swarming with Hammer Industries tech personnel making last-minute adjustments to their imminent demonstration. The front rows of seats were packed except a few chairs reserved for VIPs.

Natasha scanned the crowd again.

"Ms Potts!" she called out. Pepper and Happy saw her and started in her direction, moving with the crowd. "How was your flight?" Natalie asked when they were close enough to not have to shout.

"Fine, thank you," Pepper said.

"I'll wait for you right here, Ms Potts," Happy said. "Call if you need anything."

"I'll show you to your seats," Natasha said. Her phone rang, and

she answered it without looking at the number. "Natalie Rushman."

Tony called Natasha while he was installing the new RT in his chest, so he skipped the teleconferencing visuals. He didn't want anyone to see his chest. Purple and black streaks radiated outwards from the old RT, covering Tony's torso and crawling up his neck like bad tattoos. Sometimes when he looked at them he thought they might be moving.

Natasha answered as Natalie, still pretending to be the innocent assistant instead of the lethal S.H.I.E.L.D. operative.

But it was the S.H.I.E.L.D. operative Tony needed.

"Ivan's up to something," Tony said before she finished saying hello. "He called me from a lab. Looks like it's in a warehouse complex somewhere near the Expo."

There was the barest of pauses. "Yes, Ms Potts has just arrived," Natasha said briskly. "OK. I'll be right there."

She must already be at the Expo, Tony thought as Natasha hung up. Good. Maybe she could get the S.H.I.E.L.D. personnel who were undoubtedly creeping around the place to slow Whiplash down. Or at least be on the lookout for whatever he was planning.

Tony needed to suit up and fly to the Expo, and quick. But before he could do that, he had to get the new RT into his chest. The palladium toxicity in Tony's body had reached a point of no return. If the new RT didn't stabilize everything and give him enough strength to let his immune system start to purge the palladium, then Tony Stark was not

going to make it.

And that idea was intolerable. "Jarvis," Tony said, "let's get ready to swap in this new toy. How does that sound?"

"Marvellous, sir," Jarvis said.

Tony plugged it in.

At first, he felt as if someone had sent a mild electric shock through his entire body. His heart thumped back into action and blood started moving through his veins again. And then he felt strong.

He turned to look at himself in the mirror — and watched as something extraordinary happened. The purplish streaks darkened to a pure black. Tony's eyes popped.

Then the black streaks became fainter and began to turn silver. The silvery colour of the RT appeared to spread along the pathways where the infection had been. Then the streaks were gone.

"I did it, Dad," he whispered. There was a silence, until Jarvis broke it.

"How do you feel, sir?" the AI asked. It was an empty question, really. Tony was sure Jarvis had already run a dozen screens on Tony's metabolism and overall health without Tony's awareness.

Even if the question was motivated by simple politeness, Tony appreciated it. After all, Jarvis had been there when none of the humans of Tony's acquaintance were. Which was, of course, his fault... but now was not the time to dwell on that.

"Alive," he said.

CHAPTER 13

After her telephone call with Tony, Natasha left Pepper in the front row and headed for the exit, a plan already forming in her mind. On the way she made another call. Nick Fury answered on the first ring.

"Fury," she said. "Tell Agent Coulson to lock down the Expo."

Happy saw her coming, and she hung up before Fury could ask any questions.

"Hey," Happy said.

"I need a ride," she said. He caught the urgency in her voice and fell into step with her.

Happy drove the limo while Natalie changed into her S.H.I.E.L.D. uniform in the backseat. S.H.I.E.L.D. had traced Ivan's call to a warehouse just outside the city. Natasha Romanoff was hoping Whiplash would be there. She wanted to fight him.

But first she had to deal with Happy, who still didn't know her real name.

"So," Happy said, "I've seen you having these mysterious phone conversations for the past few weeks, and now you're changing into some sort of secret-agent outfit... So why don't you level with me?"

Natasha decided to be direct. "You want the truth, Happy? I'm a secret agent working for an organization called S.H.I.E.L.D." Natasha

kept talking as she zipped up her boots. "I was deployed to Stark Industries because your boss's behaviour is endangering the Iron Man suit and the American people. The agency sent me to LA to keep an eye on Tony and to make sure that someone was there to call in the cavalry if things got out of hand. Now step on it, Happy," she said. "Come on."

"I think maybe I'm going to stop driving people around," Happy said as he floored the limo's accelerator. He quietly accepted Natasha's explanation without questions. She was relieved.

Before the limo came to a complete stop outside the main access gate to the warehouse complex, Natasha had already opened the car door. "Wait here," she said.

"No way," Happy shot back. He turned off the ignition and got out of the limo. "You're not going in there alone."

She gave him a pitying look. "Please. Not now."

Coming around the front of the car, Happy shook his head. " 'No' is not an answer I'll accept."

"Fine," she said with a sigh.

Happy was about to ask how they were going to get into the warehouse, when Natasha walked up to an electronic access pad next to the front door and tapped in a code, as if she owned the place. She glanced at him, anticipating his question. "S.H.I.E.L.D.," she said.

Inside, they headed across a broad, multi-storey atrium—the part of the building that was for show—and reached the part of the building where the work happened. The lab looked like any other lab or hospital

in the world: sterile surfaces, neutral colours. Lots of signs telling which way to go, lots of cameras detecting who went where. "How do you know—?" Happy began.

"Where Vanko's lab is?" Natasha finished for him. "A little birdie told me."

They turned a corner and ran smack into a security guard doing his rounds. Happy's instincts kicked in before he knew it.

"You go ahead—I got this guy!" he said. "I'll be OK! Go."

She started to say something but then ran down the hall, deeper into the building, before the guard could stop her.

Happy squared off against the guard, ready to box. He hooked, he fired straight rights, he went high and low with combinations...and he realized that, unlike a lot of big guys with gym muscles, the guard could take a punch. Happy nailed him with everything he had, and the guard stayed on his feet.

Happy finally landed a solid punch, and the guard was knocked out.

"I did it!" Hap said, breathing hard. His hands felt as though he'd spent the afternoon sparring with a brick wall. Time to find that girl and make sure she hasn't gotten herself into more trouble, he thought. Happy turned to start after Natasha but stopped short in surprise.

The entire length of the hall floor between where he stood and where she waited impatiently was strewn with the unconscious bodies of at least a dozen other security personnel. Happy looked from Natasha to her handiwork and back, unable to believe that she had handled

all these guards in the time it had taken him to knock out one guy the old-fashioned way.

"Come on!" Natasha said. To her credit, she didn't comment about his boxing skills or complain that he had made her wait.

Inside the lab there were discarded prototype drones, bits and pieces of Arc Reactor models, a complete machine shop, and an incredible mess. Unused or broken parts lay on tables or where they had fallen on the floor. Cables, conduits, and hoses ran from here to there all over the space, with no visible system or guiding principle. Computers were left on, their screens displaying information that in any reasonable security regime would have been hidden away.

She dialled Tony. "He's gone," she said.

CHAPTER 14

Back at the Expo, Pepper watched as Justin Hammer strode across the polished stage to the microphone.

"Iron Man," Hammer said. "An invention that grabbed press headlines the world over. Today, though, the press has a problem on their hands. They're about to run out of ink." He arrived at centre stage. "Today I give the world Lieutenant Colonel James T Rhodes and the War Machine!"

From the ceiling, a platform descended to reveal the War Machine. Pepper caught her breath. The War Machine suit was brute strength, shining silver in the spotlights. A million flashbulbs went off.

Pepper knew that Rhodey was inside the suit. She knew, too, that he must have fought the decision to exhibit War Machine at the Expo. He was a soldier, but he did not love war; he loved his country. Like Tony, Rhodey believed that the Iron Man armour was best used only as a weapon of last resort.

Pepper could feel the adulation wafting from the crowd, and she could see Hammer eating it up. "Nifty stuff, right?" he said. Then, in a more sober tone, he added, "But in a truly perfect world, men and women of the United States military would never have to set foot on

the battlefield again." Music built, and Hammer stepped around Rhodey to the lip of the stage. "Ladies and gentlemen, today we cross the threshold into ... a perfect world."

Red, white, and blue smoke erupted around the stage as four lines of armoured soldiers marched in perfect rhythm into the Tent of Tomorrow and stopped in formation along the sides of the stage. An announcer boomed out the name of each branch of service as its members appeared in turn: "Army! Navy! Air Force! Marines!"

When they met in their formation, slowly and in unison, the thirty-two soldiers pivoted and raised their right arms in a salute to War Machine.

And that was when Pepper — along with everyone else in the Tent of Tomorrow — realized that these were not armoured soldiers.

They were walking, synchronized, remote-controlled drones.

Pepper had never heard a noise as loud as the roar of approval from the crowd. Each group of drones was coloured like the dress uniform of the service branch it represented, and each had particular design tweaks. The Air Force drones were equipped to fly, with wing-like additions to every limb and active control surfaces along their backs. The Army drones were squat and loaded with heavy weaponry. The Marine contingent was a bit leaner than its Army counterpart; the Marine drones looked ready to storm a beach right then and there, if only an enemy could be located. And the Navy drones stood streamlined and potent, midnight blue, racked and bristling with

missiles that looked capable of turning an enemy fleet to scrap metal in seconds flat.

Then, with timing so precise that Pepper would later wonder whether he had planned his arrival this way, Iron Man appeared.

Tony rocketed down through the hole in the roof in his new Mark VI suit, complete with a new triangle on the chest to match his lifesaving RT.

Whatever Hammer felt at seeing Tony crash his big party, he was a showman, and he rolled with it. "And that's not all!" Hammer said. "Here, ladies and gentlemen, is our very special surprise guest: Iron Man!"

Tony waved to the crowd while he popped open a communications channel from his heads-up display to Rhodey's HUD inside the War Machine suit. "Really?" Tony said. "A big gun on the shoulder? What ever happened to aesthetics?"

HUD to HUD, Rhodey said, "Tony—"

"That's mine," Tony said.

"It still is."

"These drones are trouble," Tony said. "Next time do your homework."

"What are you talking about?" Rhodey asked.

Tony sent him a quick scan of the drones flanking him on all sides. They were pretty well put together, and without a doubt would be a tough fight for anyone who wasn't in an Iron Man suit, but whoever

had done the primary design work hadn't cared much about hiding the specifics of the power systems.

While Tony waited for Rhodey to assess what Tony had sent him, Hammer made it clear that his enthusiasm for his special guest was flagging. "Now, if Mr Stark would step aside..."

"Oh, my goodness," Rhodey said. He had just realized what Tony already knew. That RT Tony took off Ivan Vanko in Monaco, and all the RTs in these drones?

The same.

"Go home," Iron Man told War Machine. "It's about to get ugly."

Then he commandeered the Tent of Tomorrow's loudspeaker and said, "Ladies and gentlemen, this pavilion is currently closed to the public. In an organized fashion, please find the nearest—"

He paused as he heard a ratcheting click and turned to find War Machine's heavy machine gun aimed right between his eyes. "Don't point that thing at me," he said.

"Tony," Rhodey said, HUD to HUD. "Go."

In unison, all thirty-two drones on the stage pivoted away from War Machine, dropped their salutes, and focused their array of weaponry on Iron Man.

Hammer, edging towards the wings, called to one of his technical support staff. "What is going on?"

"We're not doing it!" the tech said.

At that moment Iron Man shot upwards, and the eight Air Force

drones followed him, shattering the glass dome of the Tent of Tomorrow into a blizzard of slivers that rained down onto the crowd.

"You want to do this?" Tony yelled as he did a series of barrel rolls and zigzags through the Expo. War Machine stayed hot on his tail. "Let's do this!"

"I'm not doing this!" Rhodey yelled back. "You need to get out of here." Rhodey was a prisoner inside the suit, without any control. And the suit was going after Tony!

Not likely. "Jarvis, drone him," Tony said.

"Unable to penetrate the firewall," Jarvis said, almost apologetically.

"Do something, man!" Rhodey said.

Tony gritted his teeth. "I'm trying," he said.

The Air Force drones, meanwhile, had spread out into a kind of double-wing formation, staying tight on Iron Man. The drones were smart, well-programmed, and designed to function smoothly as a team.

"So," he said to Rhodey over the comm-link. "Still happy you ran off with my suit?"

"You want to talk about this now?" Rhodey said.

"No. But since this army of drones might actually succeed in shooting my suit down, it struck me that maybe you and I should clear the air." Tony dodged rounds of fire—some of which came from War Machine's rotating-barrel cannon. "See what I mean?"

"I'm not doing that," Rhodey said.

"You're flying around in the suit that's doing it," Tony said. "Jarvis, can you get control yet?"

"The situation is less than ideal, sir," Jarvis said. "But you may rest assured that I'm making the very best of it."

"Hey, Rhodey," Tony said. "Did I ever tell you that I was having trouble with the RT and that I was about to die because I couldn't figure out how to power it without using a substance that was slowly poisoning me?"

"As a matter of fact, you did not," Rhodey said.

"Well, it's true," Tony said. "I just thought I would let you know that I got it all figured out, and it's all good now. I'm not going to die."

"Terrific," Rhodey said. At that moment the War Machine suit fired off a missile, and for a while Tony was too busy to talk.

CHAPTER 15

A large crowd gathered in a pavilion outside the Tent of Tomorrow, and another group watched from a balcony across the Expo's main thoroughfare. All attendees agreed: it was one of the best shows Tony Stark had ever put on.

That excitement lasted until the moment when the eight Army drones in formation marched out of the Tent of Tomorrow's front entrance. They extruded stabilizers from their legs, like the legs that come out from the sides of a crane to keep it steady. Then they deployed heavy guns from racks on their shoulders and aimed the weapons skywards. The drones waited, making minuscule movements that tracked the progress of Iron Man and War Machine as they moved across the sky.

Then, as the aerial show wound back over the main Expo grounds, the Army drones fired simultaneously into the air.

Around the Expo's entrances and exits, S.H.I.E.L.D. personnel appeared. Their orders were to intercept Ivan Vanko.

Pepper tried to exit the Tent of Tomorrow through the main entrance, but a guard directed her away. "Some of those robots are out front there, ma'am," he said, pointing with his torch towards a hallway that curved around the outside of the auditorium. "You should use the

side door, over that way."

She came out of the tent into chaos. Fires were burning in some of the Expo's buildings.

Tony thundered overhead, low enough that she felt the bruising wake of his passage. Firing wildly, the Air Force drones came close behind, with Rhodey an unwilling passenger in their midst. Around Pepper, the world dissolved into explosions. She dropped to her knees. When everything had passed, she looked around again, amazed to still be alive.

"Was that Pepper?" Tony yelled.

"Ms Potts was indeed in the vicinity recently," Jarvis replied.

"Tell me she's OK, Jarvis."

"Certainly, sir," Jarvis said. "Would you like me to ascertain the truth of that statement first?"

"My display just zoomed on her," Rhodey cut in. "She looks fine."

"Your display?" Tony said. *Why would—?* he wondered. *Ah. That explains some things.* Tony knew that Ivan had designed the power source for the drones. He therefore assumed that Ivan also had programmed the drones and War Machine to seek and destroy Iron Man. If Ivan was controlling Rhodey's systems, he might also be the party responsible for checking on Pepper's status—which meant that he viewed Pepper either as a target or as leverage. That was a problem.

Right now, though, Tony's immediate problem was the eight drones on his tail. He peeled into a high loop, slowing down ever so slightly.

85

The Air Force drones closed in. He wanted to keep them close and keep their fields of fire angled away from the evacuating crowds. He hoped to spring a little surprise when the time was right.

Tony wasn't sure which feature of the Expo was his favourite: the Unisphere, reconstructed from the original built for the first Stark Expo, or the artificial lake Tony had added as a reflecting pool. Two hundred feet tall, the Unisphere rotated on a solar-powered pedestal assembly. The globe's longitude lines were I-beams, and its structural integrity was guaranteed by the stainless-steel continents and archipelagos that adorned it. A massive Stark logo stood out above the continents, angling from south to north across the Unisphere's equator.

All of this went through his mind as he flew in a high arc over the lake. War Machine was hot on his trail. "Jarvis, we need to get a handle on War Machine's operating system," Tony said.

"Displaying architecture," Jarvis said. A graphic rendering of the information architecture of the War Machine suit appeared on Tony's HUD.

Rhodey broke in. "What's going on up there, man?"

Tony dipped close to the surface of the lake, letting the violent currents of his passage kick up rooster tails of water to confuse his pursuers. At the same time, he swerved through a series of tight loops and figure of eights. He lost a couple of the Air Force drones but found himself facing three others across the length of the lake. They were steaming towards him at full thrust. The least he could do, Tony

reasoned, was reciprocate the gesture.

The impact with the centre Air Force drone was not too bad. A little shudder through the frame of the suit, a brief whiteout in the visual sensors, and then Tony was through the blossoming fireball. The Unisphere loomed in his sights, and the surviving Air Force drones— some of them, anyway; they were moving too fast for a reliable count—were closing in on his tail again.

But War Machine was closer. Tony ran a targeting projection on the Unisphere.

"This might hurt," he said to Rhodey.

"What? No, you are not—"

The way Tony had it figured, War Machine—and therefore Rhodey—was tight enough on his burners that any calculations that worked for Tony would work for Rhodey, too. The Unisphere rotated slowly.

The Mark VI Iron Man suit flew through a gap in the rotating sphere, with War Machine close behind. Tony's calculations were correct: he and Rhodey got through safely. The Air Force drones, however, didn't make the move fast enough; they smashed into the sphere.

Pepper saw the explosions and was nearly sick with worry. She took out her phone and called Tony, who answered on the third ring. "Ms Potts," he said, "I told you never to call me here."

"I just wanted to—"

Pepper heard impacts through the phone. "Ouch," Tony said. "Gotta go. Bye."

He clicked off. That's when she saw him reappear through the smoke billowing up from the Unisphere, with War Machine a few yards behind and what looked like two Air Force drones flanking them. War Machine was firing with everything it had except the big missiles. Whatever the reason for not deploying those, Pepper was glad about it.

Coming in low and hot back over the lake, Tony thought briefly that he'd lost the Air Force drones. Only War Machine showed up on the pursuit radar. Scanning the HUD for drones, Tony was shocked when he was jerked downwards by War Machine grappling along his back. The grey metal suit had caught up with him. War Machine wrenched Tony off course and sent both of them scraping along the side of a building, peeling off a floor's worth of windows and a long line of steel framing.

"Aaaah!" Tony cried out. "I will remember you did that."

They shot clear of the building, out towards the edge of the Expo grounds. Tony braked hard, pivoting him and War Machine around their collective centre of gravity. War Machine's grip on him loosened, and Tony took the opportunity to fling War Machine—with the unfortunate Rhodey inside, yelling all kinds of things on the HUD-to-HUD frequency—into the reflecting pool.

One of the gadgets he'd built into the Mark VI (despite being unconvinced he'd ever have a use for it) was a retractable spike.

"Sorry about this," he said to Rhodey as the War Machine suit hit

the deck on its back. Tony aimed the spike directly at the base of the suit's neck.

Shling!

There. He started piping Jarvis's new software through the wiring in the spike and into the onboard network. War Machine went inert. Rhodey was talking — Tony could feel the vibrations through the spike — but no sound came through because the suit was down.

"Rebooting systems," Jarvis said smoothly.

About 30 seconds later, the War Machine suit came back online, system by system. Rhodey sat up, and Tony let him. They settled next to each other on the edge of the pool, enjoying a moment of peace and quiet. About a hundred cherry trees lined the edges of the pool and the paths that circled it and wound through the gardens. "Feeling better?" Tony asked after a bit.

"I'm so sorry," Rhodey said.

CHAPTER 16

With cherry blossoms drifting around them, Tony and Rhodey took a breather. But Tony knew he had to get moving. Natasha had told him Ivan was no longer at his workshop in the warehouse. Tony hoped S.H.I.E.L.D. was doing its job and would find Whiplash before he had to.

His thoughts were interrupted when the last remaining Army drone broke the peace and quiet he and Rhodey had been enjoying. It was slightly the worse for wear, with obvious repulsor burns and scoring on its armour, but it was moving on its own two feet to carry out its mission.

Tony opened the HUD-to-HUD with Rhodey. "Well," he said. "You ready to make it up to me?"

"I think we got this," Rhodey said. They stood facing the lone drone.

Then they heard a rumble, and blossoms began to shake loose from the trees. The rumble grew louder, its vibrations coming up through the soles of their boots. Sixteen more drones surrounded them. The Marines had arrived. So had the Navy. The reinforcements landed in a precise pattern, creating crossfire but keeping each other out of the planned field of fire.

The Army drone had come in first, and it took the initiative. With a ratcheting whine, a missile rack opened out of the drone's shoulders

and snapped into position.

Tony didn't waste any time. He stepped up and reached out, tearing the rack from the drone's torso while it was still executing the firing routine. Before the drone could abort, Tony had turned around the launch tube. The missile fired, annihilating the robot's upper half and temporarily whiting out Tony's heads-up display.

He let the tube drop and said, "That's one."

Pepper was crossing the Expo grounds, trying to find Agent Coulson. She had glimpsed him earlier and knew he and his S.H.I.E.L.D. agents were trying to help. She had seen the other drones take off in Tony's direction, and she wanted the agents to help him. She tried calling Tony again. He didn't answer. "Hi, this is Tony Stark, and you're Pepper Potts," said his voicemail. Beeeeep.

Pepper spotted Coulson ahead. She started to follow, putting her phone away; then she froze, still as a rabbit. With a flash of light and a crack that rang in her ears, Whiplash appeared in front of her.

Pepper looked past him, but Coulson had already gone into the milling crowds. Even if he'd heard Ivan, he was too far away to help. And this Ivan was different, not the invader from the Monaco racetrack. This Ivan was armoured in a deranged parody of the Mark VI suit, gleaming like a gladiator, his hair loose and his face obscured behind a triangular mask. He loomed between her and safety.

"Congratulations on the new job," he said.

CHAPTER 17

Foom! One more Navy drone down. Rhodey was holding down one of the Marine drones as his weapons chewed through its armour.

"Ahoy, pal," Tony said, HUD-to-HUD. "I'm taking bets on whether we get this done before Ivan shows up to take advantage of us in our weakness."

"Well, now, that would be just like him to take advantage, wouldn't it?" Rhodey said.

They combined their fire on a Marine drone. Rhodey pinned it down and chewed it up with the big machine gun, and Tony finished it off. In the middle of this assault, Pepper called. Again, Tony's lighthearted attitude evaporated the second he saw her face. She was mortally terrified. He could read her expression, even with the lousy resolution of the heads-up image. "Pepper?"

"Tony . . ." she said. And that's when the view shifted a bit, and he saw who else was there. He understood both her terror and why she had made the call.

"Where are you going?" Rhodey shouted, HUD-to-HUD, over the shriek of explosive projectiles from the diminishing number of drones. Tony counted two Marines and four Navy drones left. From seventeen

92

to two, the odds had improved to six to one. Tony felt he had done his part.

"Keep them contained. Don't let them into the fairgrounds," Tony said, and thundered away.

Fifteen seconds later, Tony landed in front of Whiplash and Pepper. The impact was hard enough to shake the ground and cause a momentary swirl of interference across his heads-up. Vanko held Pepper in one hand, lazily flicking a whip around her feet. She was clearly terrified, but Pepper Potts was also one tough customer. She stood straight.

Tony could see that Ivan had been busy. The villain had designed himself a new suit. He had graduated to 'armouring' himself to protect his own limbs from his nasty whips. Of course, the whips were improved as well. They could be stored in spools that wrapped around the forearms. The whips deployed from slots at the insides of the wrists, and they could be controlled without the user holding them. It was as if the whips grew from Ivan, and he now used them not as tools but as extensions of his arms.

"Let her go before—" Tony started to say, and then stopped as Ivan released her. She scrambled away from him.

"Easy, wasn't it?" Ivan said. "You think I want her? No." Snap! went one of the whips. "I want only you."

"We still have a problem, then," Tony said.

Out came the full-length whips, crackling as they uncoiled and

sparked to white-hot life, melting the asphalt on contact. When Ivan came at him with the whips, Tony grabbed hold of one and used it as a pivot to fling Ivan away, smashing him into a row of barriers. Vanko started to get up, and Tony covered the distance between them quickly.

The last time he had tangled with Ivan, Tony had been wearing the portable suit from the football, and Vanko had been using an experimental prototype of his whips and the armoured frame that supported them. Now Tony was in the Mark VI, with a new RT and a new lease on life, and Vanko had taken a cue from Tony and armoured up as well. Last time had been a dry run—this time was for real.

Ivan roared and went after Tony, who met him full on, exchanging punches for slashes of the whips. Tony found out quickly, though, that whatever Ivan was using this time around, it was a lot more powerful than the whips he'd had in Monaco.

"Pepper," he said, "get out of here!"

His train of thought was derailed as a whip cracked across the face shield of the Mark VI. His HUD flared and went dark. "Jarvis," Tony warned; as he spoke, the display went live again, and Ivan Vanko filled his field of vision.

"Divert to torso projector," Tony said. He felt the energy in the suit shift and then release in an enormous burst that blew Ivan through the nearest wall. In the brief lull that followed, Tony turned to Pepper. "I told you to get out of here, Pepper!" But she was frozen in place.

Ivan Vanko hit him in the small of the back and hammered him into

the pavement hard enough to crack it. Tony spun, landing a solid elbow to the side of Vanko's head. Ivan flicked a whip that caught Tony's forearm, jerking it painfully backwards. Tony rolled with the motion, scissoring Ivan's legs out from under him and stomping on the hand that held the whip. It uncoiled, and sparks shot from the forearm of Vanko's armour.

"Are we really doing this because of something you think my dad did to your dad?" Tony asked. "And what was that thing, exactly? You think my dad stole the Arc Reactor idea, right? You've hurt innocent people. Is it their fault that your dad didn't get credit?" Tony shook his head. "It's nobody's fault but your own."

The next thing he knew, a whip snapped around his ankles, and his feet were jerked out from under him. Whiplash landed on Tony's back and flicked a whip twice around Tony's neck. He caught the tip in one hand and closed his other around the base, where it came out of his wrist armour. Then Ivan hauled back with all his strength.

Tony could feel the heat from the whip through the armour around his neck. The HUD was flashing all kinds of red signals. The whips had damaged the suit's control systems. Tony couldn't get up. He couldn't really attack Ivan. And he couldn't hold the whip away from his neck forever.

There was one thing, however, that he could do . . . Letting go of the whip with one hand, he reached towards Pepper and triggered a hidden hatch in the gauntlet. It flicked open. She was looking at him, horrified

and paralyzed with fear. "Think fast," Tony said.

The Tech-Ball shot out of the compartment behind the tiny forearm hatch. Instinctively, Pepper flung up her hand to catch it. In the milliseconds before it would have impacted the palm of her hand, the Tech-Ball adjusted the consistency of its material and changed shape, transforming from a metallic spheroid to a thin elastic hemisphere that closed around Pepper's hand and moulded to its shape. Tony had been playing with the new invention and had created something more than just a fun toy.

A burst of repulsor energy exploded from the palm of Pepper's hand. The recoil knocked her back, and she stumbled and fell as the repulsor ray hit Ivan with a full-strength blast.

For a moment, nothing else changed. Vanko's arms still bulged with the strain of holding the whip around Tony's neck, and Tony's gauntleted fingers still sparked and smoked inside the tightening noose of the whip. Then, slowly, Vanko's arms relaxed. The whip loosened, and Tony jerked it away, letting it spit and crackle on the ground.

Tony stood, letting Ivan slump to the pavement. He flipped up the face shield of the Mark VI and winked at Pepper.

"Nice shot," he said.

"Thanks," Pepper said, gasping. Both of them stood there for a moment, recovering.

"How about we go home?" she asked.

He pulled off his helmet and smiled at her. "Sounds like a plan."

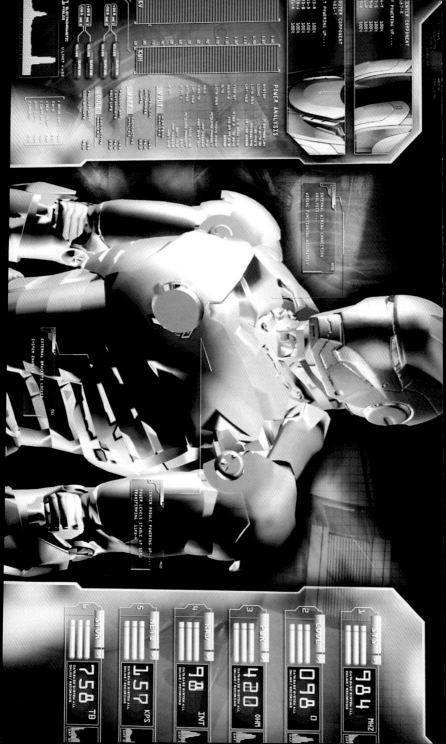